War . . . The word echoed around inside Steve ⎯ mankind's first contact with an alien life-form *really* come down to this? He'd read hundreds of science fiction novels, and had often speculated on what would happen if human beings ever really did get to meet aliens. As friends or as foes?

And, now that it was happening, he still didn't know which answer was correct. Was this war? Or some very bizarre— and alien—form of peace?

What did the Zanti *really* want? Had they been entirely honest in their dealings? And, beyond that, what did the Zanti *think*? They weren't human, apparently not even in the slightest degree. So using human thought processes to predict those of their alien . . . visitors? Invaders? What was the right word? In any event, using human models to predict Zanti behavior was likely to be unproductive, if not downright dangerous.

THE OUTER LIMITS™

THE ZANTI MISFITS

JOHN PEEL

based on the teleplay by Joseph Stefano

Tor Kids!

A TOM DOHERTY ASSOCIATES BOOK
NEW YORK

THE OUTER LIMITS #1: THE ZANTI MISFITS

Cover art by Peter Bollinger

A Tor Book
Published by Tom Doherty Associates, Inc.
175 Fifth Avenue
New York, NY 10010

Tor® is a registered trademark of Tom Doherty Associates, Inc.

ISBN: 0-812-59063-5

First edition: September 1997

Printed in the United States of America

0 9 8 7 6 5 4 3 2 1

For Jelena Tillotson
Ad "Astraea"

Throughout history, compassionate minds have pondered this dark and disturbing question: What is society to do with those members who are a threat to that society? With those malcontents and misfits whose behavior undermines and destroys the foundations of civilization?

No age, no society, has ever been free of those who chose not to belong by an act of their own will. Rebels, delinquents, revolutionaries, criminals . . . call them what you will, they have chosen not to be a part of society, and to attack the society they have rejected.

Different ages have found different answers to this question of how to treat these outlaws. Misfits have been burned, or branded, or banished. In our day, criminals are placed in jails, separated from the society they have rejected. Most such institutions are humane. Some are not. And, in extreme cases, the offender is executed.

But, like so many problems, this one is not confined to the narrow boundaries of our Earth. Other worlds face the same problem—and some have come up with drastically different solutions.

The planet known as Zanti is one where compassion and concern have been elevated to a state we humans have never known. The majority of the population there is calm, content and caring. Crime is virtually unknown, and almost everyone is very happy. Almost . . .

Even there, there are those who refuse to be a part of society. And so something had to be done to solve the problem of the Zanti misfits. . . .

CHAPTER 1

"THEY'RE AFTER US, man."

Jason turned around, his face damp with sweat, a tic in his cheek betraying his nervous state. He wiped his sticky palms against his dirty jeans, and then repeated the action. "They're getting closer all the time. I knew we were dangerous, Ben, but I never imagined that they'd send the *army* after us. What are we going to do?"

"You," Ben said dreamily, "are going to shut that stupid mouth up, that's what you're going to do." He moved to the boarded-over window. "Let me see."

Lisa watched the two youths as they changed places. They were a complete contrast, two young thugs thrown together by chance and opportunity. Ben Garth was tall, thin, sandy-haired and dark-eyed. He was like a stick of dynamite whose fuse was almost gone, sparkling brightly, ready to explode any second. His life was filled with casual, unthinking violence.

Jason Marsh was stubbier, dark-skinned and nervous. He was driven by greed; otherwise he'd never have stayed with Ben. Jason had an insatiable desire for money that had been born in his deprived childhood. Violence made him queasy, and everything made him scared.

"They can't be looking for us," Ben said simply, having stared out of the small gap for long enough. "They don't send the army to catch petty thieves."

"Petty thieves and *killers*," Lisa drawled slowly, enjoying watching Jason squirm at the last word. "Maybe they think you're as mean a dude as you believe, Ben," she added helpfully. "Maybe the police are too scared to come after you alone."

"It's nothing to do with us," Ben insisted calmly. "There must be some other reason why they're here."

"It doesn't much matter," Jason said nervously. "They're searching for *something*. And if they find us, they'll find the money. And the gun. And they'll *know* . . ."

Lisa barely glanced at where the gun lay on the small, rickety table. Only one bullet had been fired, and it was now most likely in a police file in Sacramento. It would have been taken from the bank teller during the autopsy.

She avoided thinking about that day. There was no point to it now. She had been driving the car, and had heard the shot fired, and then Ben and Jason had come running from the bank, money bags in hand, and the gun still smoking. There had been a smile on Ben's face, one that had not left his face for more than a few minutes since.

He had *enjoyed* shooting the poor teller, who'd been too slow in handing over the cash. Ben had never told her whether it had been a man or a woman he'd shot, and she'd never had the nerve to ask. Jason wouldn't even talk about the day. He had nightmares over it at least twice a week.

And the whole thing had been caught on security cameras.

Police all over California had to have a description of Ben and Jason by now. Maybe, for all she knew, of her as well. Someone might have seen her sitting in the car, waiting. She was used to being noticed, after all. She was blond, slender, tanned, and turned eyes and heads wherever she went. So maybe she was being hunted as an accessory to murder. . Among other things.

Faced with no other options, they ran, just as far as they dared. Ben seemed to have been expecting something like this for a while, because he'd stockpiled food in the trunk of the car over the course of his more or less successful raids on convenience and liquor stores before the bank raid. He'd known of this abandoned mining cabin, way up in the foothills, away from any town. Here, he'd insisted, they would be safe for as long as their supplies held out. Nobody ever came here.

Until the first army patrol came through a week ago.

Ben seemed to be warned by some dark instinct, for he had insisted that their car be hidden in the old mine workings. And the hut in which they were staying had a hidden basement, where the three of them had stayed, hardly daring to breathe, while the soldiers had tramped through the area searching for . . . what? Them? Someone else? Something else?

Then some of Ben's precautions seemed to have made sense. He had insisted on burying the cans and bottles from their meals inside the mine so as to leave no traces. It was as if he'd been expecting to be hunted all along. And perhaps, Lisa realized, he had. Given his lifestyle, sooner or later he was bound to be in trouble with the law.

That had been one of the things about him that had originally appealed to her, after all. But now? Now she was no longer so sure.

And now the soldiers were back.

Ben moved to the trapdoor in the floor, pausing only to ask Jason, "There are no cans left around, are there?"

"None at all," Jason replied. "We ate the last yesterday. There's none left now. We have to get more food, Ben."

Smiling unconcernedly, Ben said, "Not now, Jason." He held up the trapdoor. "Down." He spoke as if Jason were his pet dog. Without a murmur, Jason scurried into the hole. Then Ben turned to face Lisa. "You too."

For just a moment, anger flared inside her, making her warm and strong. What right did he have to speak to her like that? Then she saw the steel in Ben's eyes, and knew that his apparent amusement went no further than the edges of his mouth. Wordlessly, she followed Jason down. After a moment, Ben joined them, pulling down the trapdoor and locking it.

This must have been some prospector's cabin back at the turn of the century, or even earlier. Lisa had speculated that this bolt-hole was where the grizzled, half-crazed old man must have hidden to escape marauding bands of Indians. She didn't know that for sure, of course, but it made the place seem more romantic than the truth—it was a dirty, smelly little hole in the ground, with barely room for the three of them to lie and wait.

Lisa remembered the gun on the table, and smiled to herself. Had Ben made a mistake at last? If a soldier came into the cabin and saw that, then he would know that someone was around. If the soldiers *really* searched, they would find this hideaway without too much trouble. Then, in the darkness next to her, Lisa heard a metallic click, and knew that Ben had not forgotten the weapon—and that he had just readied it for possible use.

A few moments later, the cabin door opened. She heard footsteps on the rickety floor over her head, and a voice calling out, "Is there anyone here?"

For a very brief second, Lisa thought about answering. She was getting more than tired of her life right now. Even the possibility—or, rather, the certainty—that she would go to jail if she were found didn't really seem too terrible to her right now. It would have to be better than staying with Ben. But then she remembered the gun, and knew that if she made a sound, the soldier in the room above would die.

The only part of her almost-dead conscience that still prickled her was the thought of the teller who had been killed. Lisa had wanted a complete break from her old life, but never at the price of the life of another human being. To cause Ben to kill again was beyond her.

In a strange way, the knowledge of that was some sort of relief to her. Maybe she wasn't yet entirely a lost soul. Maybe there was some hope for her?

But she knew, in her heart, that this wasn't true. She'd made her choice, and now she would have to live with it, no matter how painful it might prove to be. And, with Ben, pain was a given.

The footsteps overhead started up again, and then there was the sound of the door closing. The soldier had left, going elsewhere. That was odd. Twice now, the army had passed through here, making no more than a cursory search each time. It was as if they weren't actually expecting to find anyone, but had orders to look anyway.

What was going on?

A few moments later, she heard Ben unfastening the catch, and then there was light once more as he opened the trapdoor. "Stay here," he told them. "I'll check." He moved out of the hideaway and the door came down again.

Jason whimpered slightly beside her. Naturally, he was afraid of the dark, and enclosed spaces. Lisa felt a flare of contempt, and then realized how wrong she was. When he was a child, Jason had been punished by being beaten and then locked in a closet for hours on end. He still had nightmares about that.

"It's okay," she said, trying to sound sympathetic. "We'll be out of here in a minute."

"I can't take this anymore," he whispered back. "I got to get out of here."

"It'll just be a minute," she repeated.

"Not *here*," he said, meaning the hole. "Out of this whole thing. I'm going crazy out here. And there's no food or drink or anything left. Even Ben's got to see we can't stay any longer."

"Even Ben can see that," said Ben's voice from over their heads. "Come on out."

Lisa let Jason stumble out first. In some ways, it felt kind of nice down here. Was this what being dead would be like? Lying in a dark hole in the ground, where life couldn't get at you anymore? Maybe she should just stay here, and—

"Out!" ordered Ben, in his final-warning voice.

With a sigh, Lisa clambered out of the hole. Ben let the trapdoor down gently. "Are they gone?" she asked, more for a need to speak than anything else.

"Not quite," Ben replied. He gestured to the boarded-over window. "Take a look."

Puzzled, she did so, having to elbow a frightened Jason out of the way. Placing her eye to the crack in the wood, she stared out at the hot desert landscape.

A soldier—perhaps the one who'd been in this shack a while earlier—was helping to unload supplies from the back of a truck some fifty feet down the road. These included a radio transmitter, canteen and some food. Lisa's skin went cold.

"What's going on?" she asked in a quiet voice.

"They're not going away this time," Ben said cheerfully. "They're leaving someone on guard."

"We're trapped," gasped Jason, shaking. "They're going to find us."

"There's only one place he can be planning on staying," Lisa pointed out. "And that's this cabin. We can't stay here any longer."

"No," agreed Ben. "We've got another reason to make a run for it now—aside from Jason's stomach." The door was behind them, on the far side of the cabin from where the truck was being unloaded. "We're going to have to head for the mine while they're too busy to see us. As soon as the truck moves on, we'll make a break for it."

"And if we're spotted?" asked Jason nervously.

Ben smiled and patted his gun.

Lisa felt sick. Ben was actually looking forward to this trouble. He always loved living on the edge. This whole setup must be making him very happy, in his warped and twisted fashion.

She didn't feel that way at all. There was a cold knot of fear inside her stomach that seemed to be weighing her down. Why were the soldiers here in the first place? What was happening?

What had they stumbled into?

CHAPTER 2

FURTHER OUT IN the same desert lay the ruins of a ghost town. Nothing moved there but the tumbleweeds, tossed on their restless way by the hot desert wind. Nothing, it seemed, had moved there since the last inhabitants had moved away a century earlier, looking for a less isolated and desolate place to live and die.

Fallen in the road, bleached by the sun, an old sign lay fading away with the town itself. Barely discernible on the boards were the words MORGUE, CALIFORNIA. EST. 1859— POP. 827

But the final departee from this bleak town had taken paint and crossed through the figure. Over it, he or she had painted a shaky, sloppy 0.

Now the town was owned by no one, claimed by no one, cared for by no one. The buildings were eroding, faster than the rocks. None of them seemed to hold any intact glass. Hitching rails had collapsed, horse troughs filled with weeds and brackish water—when there was any water to be found. The road, unpaved, was cracked and blistered from long years of heat and neglect.

It was a town deserted even by its ghosts, left alone to rot in the desert sun.

Steve Grave surveyed the wreckage with a slight smile from the back of the car that had brought him here. It had been a pretty comfortable ride, with the air-conditioning turned on full. He wasn't looking forward to climbing out into the dry, hot air. "You know all the nicest places, Major," he commented, running a hand through his thick, long dark hair.

Major Hill didn't really approve of him. That much had been clear throughout their long and virtually silent drive. Hill was a career man, one of those people with a commitment that went beyond zeal for his job. His uniform was exactly right, not a crease in sight, the tie precisely knotted and in place, his insignia polished and gleaming in the sunlight. His blond hair was clipped regulation short, and his eyes and face were tense and poised for action.

"This is the only place to observe events," he replied.

Of course. Steve smiled to himself again. Everything in Hill's life clearly had its place, and its purpose. Even a ghost town could have its uses.

Even a slightly scruffy, very young professor of communications could have his uses. Otherwise Hill wouldn't be here now. Steve couldn't help being amused by the rigidity of the major's attitudes. He couldn't imagine what Hill might consider doing for fun. If he even believed in such a thing.

"Well, it's not getting any cooler out there," Steve said. "If this is as far as we go, I guess we'd better go."

Hill nodded, turning off the car's engine. The air-conditioning died with it, and Steve knew it was just his imagination that made it seem like the temperature rose ten degrees immediately. He reached over the back of his seat to where he'd placed his bags in the back of the sedan.

"Let me," offered Hill, reaching over to help. It was more out of politeness than a desire to save Steve any effort.

Steve gripped his laptop. "I'll keep this," he said firmly, allowing Hill to take his briefcase. "What about the clothing in the trunk?" He'd been advised that this assignment might well last several days.

"It'll be taken to your room," the major answered.

Steve surveyed the town outside. "I hope it's in better repair than the majority of this place," he commented.

"It is," Hill answered, no trace of humor in his voice. "Certain sections have been rebuilt." He opened the door, and it wasn't just Steve's imagination that a wave of heat swept inside the car. Steeling himself, he opened his own door and stepped out into the dust of the town.

Heat battered down upon him, and only the warm breeze seemed to stir. Steve looked around. Across the road was a faded building. The sign was still legible—LIN WU CHINESE LAUNDRY—but the building was crumbling and deserted. Turning, he looked at the old hotel outside of which they had stopped. THE PALACE, read the logo, but it looked to be far from that.

He followed Hill into the shade of the second-story balcony, which cut down on the glare but did nothing about the heat. Steve had been expecting to see batwing doors, like those in a John Wayne movie, and he'd been looking forward to pushing them open, marching inside and ordering a shot of red-eye from a ghostly barkeep.

Instead, there was a cold steel door in the doorway, and a small panel set in its center. This was surprisingly high-tech for a ghost town, and he knew it was the mark of the military. The rest of the building was as dilapidated and rotting as the rest of the town; only this doorway and the car parked in the street showed any sign of the twentieth century at all.

Hill marched up to the door—Steve was amused; Hill *never* simply walked anywhere—and then pressed his hand against the panel in the door. "Hill, Major Roger," he announced.

There was a very faint whine, and the panel glowed slightly. Steve frowned, realizing that the panel was a device for scanning Hill's handprint. "High security for a deserted town," he commented.

"You can never be too secure," Hill replied.

No, thought Steve *I guess you can't be.* But it seemed like overkill to him. In fact, it seemed like the military to him. It was one reason he'd refused to follow in his father's footsteps and enlist. His father had been disappointed, but when he knew he'd never have a son who'd make it to five-star general—or whatever the ranks were—Lieutenant Colonel Barry Grave (Retired) had backed Steve's own career choice of communications. But, despite all this, Steve had known his father had been disappointed. But there was nothing he could do about having let his father down; there was no way on this Earth he'd have ever been able to take all this military precision and redundant security.

The door opened, but instead of being invited inside, Steve was greeted by the sight of the business end of a rifle. "ID," the guard behind it snapped.

Hill handed over his own card, and then stared significantly at Steve. Feeling rather foolish, Steve fumbled in his pocket for the card he'd been issued at the start of this trip and handed it across to the guard. Wordlessly, the guard retreated and shut the door on them again.

Another long wait . . . and for what? Why would he be here, accompanied by Major Roger Hill, if he weren't supposed to be? He wished they would simply cut through this nonsense and let them inside. But the military did everything in its own way and at its own speed. Steve turned his back deliberately on the door and scanned the building on the far side of the street. Next to Lin Wu's extinct laundry was Junkin's Shaving Parlor and Bath House. Steve rubbed at the stubble on his chin. If only that place were open right now! He could do with a nice, long soak.

Hill waited impassively, his attention focused inwardly. Steve knew the major was in no mood for conversation. Perversely, he was.

"History has been recorded in some pretty morbid places, Major," he commented, looking along the street. "But when a historian named Grave finds himself in a ghost town called Morgue . . ." He broke off, grinning. The thought amused him, though it clearly didn't affect the soldier in the same fashion. "Why would anyone want to call their town Morgue?" he wondered. "Some sick sense of humor? Or a macho display of pride at how tough you had to be to live here?" He broke off talking, seeing that Hill's attention had snapped upward, to the sky. Steve followed his gaze, but there was nothing at all to be seen. "Did you see it?" he asked, his stomach suddenly twisting as he realized that the moment might be upon them even now.

"I thought I did," Hill said softly. "Probably just a desert bird."

Probably . . . but who could be sure right now? Steve scanned the skies again, still seeing nothing. Then he turned back to the major. "You don't think they'll land in broad daylight, do you?"

Hill gave him a cold stare. "Why not?" he asked. "They have no reason to be afraid of us." He returned his attention to the sky. Almost as an afterthought, he added, "I wish we could feel the same about them."

That was what was bothering Steve, to be honest. "Ordinarily," he commented, "I don't ask the military any questions. I know they have their own reasons for what they do. But I can't help but wonder why we're allowing this to happen.''

He seemed to have finally hit upon the right note to start Hill talking. ''Allowing?'' the major repeated bitterly. ''We weren't given any choice, Professor. We were *told* when the penal ship would land, and then we were *ordered* to keep out of its way. No interference with their plan—or else.''

This was something that had not been included in Steve's preliminary briefing. Worrying now, he asked, ''Or else *what*? Did they say?''

Hill finally managed a cynical smile. ''Oh, they *assured* us they didn't want to have to attack us. They wanted this to be a *nonhostile sequence*. That's the way they put it. And *then* they let us know in clear and definite terms that they would not hesitate to attack, totally and effectively, if anything interfered with their plan.''

Steve realized that Hill was both angry and scared. It was a curious combination in a soldier, but he had obviously been forced to obey commands that he did not approve of and would wish changed. Giving in to the demands of the Zanti clearly didn't sit well with the major. And since they knew so very little about the Zanti . . . ''I wonder what they're like,'' Steven mused, scanning the sky, hoping to get a glimpse of their ship as it arrived. They didn't even have a clue as to what these aliens might look like.

''From our viewpoint, Professor,'' Hill answered, ''they're either suprahuman or subhuman.''

Steve nodded slightly, resting his hand gingerly on the hotel railing. It didn't give way under the strain, so he leaned on it slightly more, glad for the support. The Zanti were the very first alien species the human race had ever contacted. Well, actually, it was the other way around. The Zanti had contacted the human race. Signals they had beamed across space had been picked up by the huge radio telescope in Arecibo. They had been clearly sent by some intelligent species, and this had excited everyone working on SETI—the Search for Extraterrestrial Intelligence. Finally, *proof* of extraterrestrial life. The signals had proved to be precisely what scientists had been hoping for, scientific data and a whole mountain of information that had enabled a translation program to be established. The news had electrified the world—the human race was no longer alone in the universe!

And then—nothing. NASA and the military had clamped down on any further news about the signals or about the Zanti. Nobody heard anything for several months. Steven had been irritated by the blackout, as had most of the rest of the world, but nothing could be done about it. He had heard nothing at all about the Zanti since this first contact—until yesterday.

There was a slight movement beside his hand on the rail, and he bent to examine it. A small black ant was crawling up the post, close to his fingers. Probably disturbed by all the activity, Steve knew. After all, before the military moved in, this had been their town. They probably wanted it back. Tough. He flicked his fingers, sending the ant spinning away through the air. The ants had no say in the matter. If the human race wanted this town back, they'd take it. The ants would have to live with this decision, or die.

A bit like the fact that the human race had to live with the Zanti decision . . .

"Or," he said softly, "maybe they're simply nonhuman."

Before Hill could reply, the door behind them swung open. Steve turned, and saw a second soldier emerge and head wordlessly to the parked car. The first man held out their ID cards. Steve and Hill reclaimed them and slid them back into their pockets.

"I'm having your car parked in the stable behind the building, sir," the guard informed Hill. The stillness of the air was disturbed by the car's engine starting up again. The guard gestured toward the door. "The general is waiting for you, Professor Grave."

Steve nodded, and entered through the door. Hill followed close behind, and the guard closed and locked the outer door once again. There was a small lecternlike affair beside the door. The guard tapped a sequence of keys on a panel set into the top of it. They stood in a very small lobby, capable of holding only another two people without crowding. Opposite the door they had entered was a second door, obviously locked electronically. When the guard finished his sequence of numbers, there was a soft electronic sigh, and this door slid softly open.

"You can go through now," the guard informed them.

Steve gripped his laptop as if it were a shield, and then walked through the door. There he stopped in amazement.

He had stepped out of a John Wayne film now and into a set from *Star Wars*.

The old saloon bar was almost invisible beneath and behind all of the electronic equipment crowded into the place. Steve was no technical expert by any means, and a lot of what he was looking at didn't make a great deal of sense to him. Still, there was absolutely no mistaking some of it.

There were over a dozen consoles set up in the center of the room, with bare cables running across the floor to a generator out in the back room, Steve guessed. The wires were covered with plastic treads to keep them in place and to avoid anyone tripping over them. Technicians and other operators, all in military uniforms, manned the consoles. "Manned" was the best word for it; Steve saw only two women among the more than two dozen people bent over their instruments or scurrying about the room.

One instrument was clearly a high-powered radar device. There was no confusing the familiar sweep and beeping that he'd seen in dozens of movies. This one looked a lot more sophisticated than any he'd ever seen portrayed before, though. There was a communications desk, with several dozen phones, including one in a very conspicuous red color. There were several large computers, and other pieces of equipment that he couldn't identify at all.

To the left of the room were two large maps. One was vertical, made in some kind of very rigid plastic, and was obviously a star chart. The other lay atop a table, and was less obvious from where he stood.

The technicians all ignored him totally, and the hum of their conversations and general work noises merged with the electronic hum of the panels to create a background murmur of noise.

Steve felt a tightening of his stomach muscles. What *had* he agreed to become a part of?

CHAPTER 3

AGAIN, LISA COULD see that there was a thin grin of anticipation on Ben's thin face. *He's hoping there will be trouble,* she realized, and knew what would happen if there was. She had been drawn to Ben in the first place because of the edge of danger in his manner. Now she knew that she was paying the price for that foolish attraction. She'd been sucked down to a level of life unimaginable to her just a few months ago.

But at least she was no longer bored. Scared, yes, and repelled; but not bored.

"Okay," Ben said softly, his eyes pressed to the board, "they're all busy right now. Lisa, go first. Straight out the door, run fast and stay low. Jason, give her five seconds and then follow." He didn't even look back to see whether they were agreeing or not. Nobody in their right minds argued with him. Especially not if they wanted to keep their minds inside their skulls, where they belonged.

Well, what other option did she have but to obey? If she gave herself up now, or was caught, it would be prison for her. Having two of the wealthiest parents in the state wouldn't affect her chances in court—except negatively. She opened the door as silently as possible, and looked at the stretch of sunbaked, parched earth between her and the mine opening. It sloped downhill at this point, so the first few yards were the only ones she might be seen crossing. Bending low, she took a deep breath and then sprinted as fast as she could.

Any second, she expected to hear a cry of alarm from behind her. Heart beating, blood singing, she raced across the hard ground, sweat pouring from her—due partly to the heat, partly to nerves. It couldn't have taken her more than thirty seconds to reach the welcoming shade of the mine entrance, but it seemed like an hour. She collapsed inside, panting heavily, wiping the sweat from her brow on the back of her hand. Heaving and scared, she glanced back the way she had come. She saw Jason, scampering like an insect, in her wake, and behind him, Ben. Naturally, he hadn't bothered to hunch over as he ran. He was defying fate, or destiny, or God, or whatever—if anything—he believed in outside of himself. If he was spotted, then so be it. He was a crazy fool, but he was also lucky.

They were all three together then, breathing hard and looking back. There was no sign of any movement from the cabin. The truck and the soldiers were no longer visible from this angle.

"Now what?" asked Lisa, trying to act nonchalant.

"We wait for the truck to leave," Ben replied. "Then we make a run for it in the car." He shaded his eyes, and gestured. "Into the desert, I think. If we cross it, we can head into Nevada and hit the first town we find for stores."

"I'm getting thirsty already," Jason said.

"Save your thirst," Ben replied. "It's going to be a long

drive, and I don't want one complaint from you. Understand me?''

Jason licked his lips and then nodded nervously.

Lisa turned away. Ben enjoyed humiliating Jason, as he enjoyed humiliating everyone. He simply enjoyed exercising his power, for any excuse. Or none. It might just as easily be her that he picked on next. Ben was an equal opportunity offender.

After a short wait, they heard the unmistakable sound of the truck firing up, and then leaving. Whatever those soldiers were doing here, they were certainly busy. Something odd was happening, but Lisa didn't care to know any more about it. All that bothered her right now was getting out of here. It would be wonderful to get some fresh clothes, to have a shower, to eat a good meal. She'd not expected to become a fugitive, and had only packed an overnight bag. Her clothing was in a dreadful state, and she knew that she must wash them. Being on the run hadn't given her much time to shop. The first motel they found, she wanted to get a room and really clean up.

''Right,'' said Ben. ''Let's get the car ready. While that soldier's busy, we should be able to make a run for it.''

Steve knew he was staring, but he couldn't help it. He felt as if he'd walked into the middle of a science fiction movie. In one way, he supposed he had—except this was real, and not just a film set.

''I'll be at my desk,'' Hill said softly from behind his shoulder. ''It's over there, if you want me for anything.'' He held up the briefcase he was carrying. ''I'll put this on yours. It's the next one over.'' He started across the room toward the desks he'd indicated. They were at the far side of the room, by another door.

Steve followed him slowly across the room. All around, the

operators and technicians were working on the panels, ignoring his progress. He had very little idea of what most of them were doing, but they were all moving precisely, obviously going through a familiar routine. One person did catch his eyes, a youngster barely out of his teens. The youth grinned quickly, then turned back to his work, Steve already forgotten.

At the far side of the room was an incongruous beaded curtain. Steve imagined that it had once separated the main body of the saloon from a poker parlor. He could imagine well-dressed gamblers, dark-suited and white-shirted, with hats, neat mustaches, jewelled cuff links and hidden derringers walking the path he'd just taken, but some hundred years in the past. Into a smoky, dangerous and perhaps lucrative gambling den. He stepped through the curtain, and his illusion was shattered instantly.

Now the room held only four desks and a couple of vending machines. Hill was at one desk, and another had Steve's case laid across it. The other two were mussed up, with papers, reports and computers on them, but without occupants. The only other person in the room was at one of the vending machines, struggling to free a cola can from its maw.

Steve couldn't repress a smile. This was, somehow, the archetypal view he had of General Maximilian Hart. His father's best friend, and "Uncle Max" as he'd been until Steve was in his teens. Hart was one of those men who looked exactly what he was—tall, muscular, even at his age, with short, iron-gray hair and piercing blue eyes. Every line of his body told you that this was a man used to being in command.

And he was utterly useless with anything smacking of technology. He could break VCRs, cause computer hard drives to crash—and vending machines to hang grimly on to their wares. The irony of such a man being in charge of one of the most technology-heavy assignments in the history of the U.S. armed forces wasn't lost on Steve. Quietly, he crossed the room, reached in and pulled the cola can from the machine. He held it out to the general with a smile.

Hart looked up and saw him, and his frown at the machine changed to a delighted grin. "Steve!" he exclaimed, straightening up and accepting the can. Then he put it down on the machine and gave Steve a hug. "You're twenty-four hours late," he scolded.

Steve shrugged and then sighed. "I was *supposed* to have been here two days ago to begin work. I was in Washington for my preliminary briefing when some five-star personality decided that this event might be better covered by a commissioned officer."

Hart winced. "I thought we'd already resolved that," he muttered. "You were always the logical choice for this assignment. And not just because I like you. Your qualifications and background make you perfect." Then he held up a hand, smiling. "I know, this is your story. Obviously, you made it here, so what happened?"

Steve grinned back. "I replied that commissioned officers *make* history. Musty young professors record it."

Hart snorted with amusement. Steve noticed that Hart seemed to have forgotten about the cola can he'd been fighting the machine for. Steve hadn't; the heat had made him thirsty, so he pulled a dollar bill of his own out and fed it to the machine.

"I guess this makes you a new kind of . . . war correspondent, Steve," Hart said softly, picking his words carefully. "The first of the interplanetary kind."

Steve pulled his own can out, and looked up at his father's old friend with worry. "Is that it?" he asked. "Is it really war?"

"In a manner of speaking, I guess it is." Hart finally picked up his cola, gestured at the beaded curtain, and then led the way back out of the small room and into the main area. "And this is the new kind of battlefield. All computerized, run by machines and not men. It's not nearly as messy as the old kind of war. Computers don't bleed.''

War . . . The word echoed around inside Steve's brain. Had mankind's first contact with an alien life-form *really* come down to this? He'd read hundreds of science fiction novels, and had often speculated on what would happen if human beings ever really did get to meet aliens. As friends or as foes?

And, now that it was happening, he still didn't know which answer was correct. Was this war? Or some very bizarre— and alien—form of peace?

Well, that was why he was here—to record the events for posterity. Oh, there were security cameras on the walls monitoring what happened here, but simple facts don't always tell you what you need to know about an event. The human factor complicates matters. And, in this case, the alien factor certainly would.

What did the Zanti *really* want? Had they been entirely honest in their dealings? And, beyond that, what did the Zanti *think*? They weren't human, apparently not even in the slightest degree. So using human thought processes to predict those of their alien . . . visitors? Invaders? What was the right word? In any event, using human models to predict Zanti behavior was likely to be unproductive, if not downright dangerous.

Hart led him to one of the consoles. It was the one Steve had already identified as the radar, and the technician was the young man Steve had spotted earlier. He looked up with a faint smile, which was wiped from his face when he saw that Steve was accompanied by the general.

''Have you made radar contact with the Zanti yet?'' Steve asked.

Hart shook his head. ''Not yet. And we can scan up to low orbit with the equipment we have here. We're also patched into a comsat''—he gestured at the next console, and the female operator there—''that is supposed to warn us when they're approaching. So far, nothing.''

Looking at the screen, Steve asked, ''Are you sure we can even detect them? I mean, we've got some pretty sophisticated stealth aircraft ourselves. Who knows what kind of technology the Zanti have?''

''Nobody,'' said Hart gravely. ''And that's the problem. The only things we know about the Zanti are what they've told us themselves. And we're not stupid in the military, Steve, contrary to some popular views on the matter. We know that the Zanti have told us only as much as they want us to know. So . . . could they be here and we can't see them? It's a distinct possibility. But the Zanti gave us their word that we would know when they were coming. And that's all we have to go on.''

''Do you believe them?'' asked Steve.

''We *have* to believe them,'' Hart said bluntly. ''Otherwise . . .'' He shrugged, then stood slightly taller. ''Gentlemen!'' he called out loudly. ''And ladies,'' he added, nodding at the satcom operator.

The noise and bustle in the room calmed down very quickly. Everyone turned to look at the general, who gestured toward Steve. ''I want you all to take a good look at Professor Steven Grave. He is this country's Official Historian of Interplanetary Contact.'' He managed a small grin, and asked Steve, ''Did I get that title right?'' There was a small amount of subdued laughter, and Steve smiled as he nodded. ''Good; you know how fussy we are in the military about getting titles right.'' This brought some more subdued laughter. ''What does this mean?'' he asked the assembled soldiers. ''It means that he's going to be observing everything and everyone. That he's going to be asking all kinds of nontechnical questions. And that he's going to be writing down everything he hears and sees and thinks. He's been cleared by SAC, NASA, the War Department and probably a few organizations we don't even know about. Congress has ratified him, the taxpayers are paying him and I like him. If he gets in your hair, don't brush him out. And if he asks you questions, you are allowed to answer with more than your name, rank and serial number. That's all. Thank you.''

There was further polite laughter, and everyone returned to their previous levels of noise and activity. Hart clapped Steve cheerfully on the back, and then led him once again through the beaded curtain. He gestured to the desk where Steve's briefcase sat.

''That'll be yours for as long as you need it, Steve,'' he said. ''Take a few minutes to get it the way you like it. Then feel free to talk to anyone you like about whatever you like. I know I don't have to tell you to stay out of the way if anything happens, and I can't think of any other warnings I might give you that you'd be at all inclined to listen to.''

Steve grinned. ''Thanks—I think.'' He laid his laptop down on the desk, and pushed aside the keyboard of the computer that already sat there. ''I'll use my own machine, thanks.''

Hart snorted. ''You're a sentimentalist, Steve. That machine you're turning down is state of the art.''

''So sue me.'' Steve started to unpack his case, removing his cassette recorder and pocketing several blank tapes before loading one into the machine, ready for when he conducted interviews. ''I get it from my father, I imagine. You know how sentimental he could get at times.'' He paused a moment, recalling some of those days himself. His father had loved big Labor Day barbecues, Yankee ball games, sailing . . . and the military, with a passion. ''But even he'd find it hard to come to grips with a war when your enemy can come out of interplanetary space. And may look like something from a nightmare.''

"Now, just a minute, Steve," Hart said urgently. "So far as we know, the inhabitants of the planet Zanti are not our enemies."

For the first time in a while, Hill spoke up, his voice tinged with bitterness. "They're not our friends." He caught Steve's eye and continued. "According to all the self-help books I've ever read, friends don't coerce friends."

Steve saw the angry look in Hart's eyes and realized that the two men must have been continuing this disagreement for about as long as they had worked together on this project. Both of them were committed, but apparently to diametrically opposing viewpoints. He had a certain amount of sympathy for both attitudes, but knew better than to make a decision yet. He needed more information first.

"My father once told me," Steve said gently, "that the thing which made Max Hart a great general was that he almost liked his enemy. Not that this meant he wouldn't try to kill them, or die trying."

Hart's eyes shone. "When you don't feel for your enemy, you don't respect him. And when you don't respect him, your judgment is flawed. You either overrate or underrate him." He paused, rubbing his chin thoughtfully. "You've been shown the transcripts of the Zanti government's first messages to us, Steve. Would *you* call it coercion?"

His memory ranged back at the eyes-only papers he'd been shown. Page after page of them, all from the Zanti government. And all filled with the same, insistent statements. "Yes," he said without hesitation. "The kind that makes me want to grab a rifle, stand outside there and fight for my country. My *world*." He saw a measure of approval in Hill's eyes at this comment.

Shaking his head, Hart moved closer to them both. "Grabbing rifles and going off to fight is a thing of the past, Steve. War with another planet would be another kind of war altogether. It would be fought with lasers, killer satellites and bombs. The individual foot soldier is as obsolete in such a war as a dinosaur.'' He rubbed his chin again. ''We've had a small army of psychologists, psychiatrists and xenobiologists go over those transcripts dozens of times, to try to squeeze every last drop of information from them that we can. Their belief is that the Zanti are a discipline-oriented society. They're perfectionists who like everything to be just so, without deviation. They can't tolerate anything that misses the mark of their own expectations. That's why their communication looks like coercion—to them, we should simply understand that what they state is *right*, and go along with it. They're not used to discussion, or to explaining themselves.''

''Very narrow-minded of them,'' Steve commented.

''Maybe,'' agreed Hart. ''But if we can be more flexible, then we should. Because they seem to be as unwilling as we are to start total war. Even though they *know* they'd win. And—the really scary part, Steve—even though *we* know they'd win. . . .''

CHAPTER 4

LISA SAT IN the passenger seat of their Thunderbird, nervously awaiting whatever Ben had planned. Jason was in the back, scrunched forward, leaning on the backs of the two front seats. Ben stood in the entrance to the mine, staring out.

"What's he planning?" asked Jason. "What are we going to do?" He shook his head. "I hate the thought of the army being after us. The police are bad enough—but who wants the army on their tails?"

"Calm down, Jason," Lisa said, trying to sound less worried than she was. "I'm sure Ben's got some plan in mind."

"Yeah," agreed Jason. "Like he had when we hit the bank. And we've been holed up weeks after *that* plan."

Lisa turned and glared at him. "You want to get out and go on your own?" she asked sweetly.

Swallowing, Jason shook his head. "I didn't mean anything by it," he said. "I was just nervous. You . . . you wouldn't tell Ben what I said, would you?"

"No," Lisa informed him honestly. There was no need. Ben already knew just how unreliable Jason was. The only thing that had kept Jason in line so far was his greed for money. The proceeds from their robbery had been gnawing at his mind all the time they'd been hiding out. Jason itched to spend the cash, and the pain of that itch was driving him crazy. She wondered briefly if he knew that the money was now stashed in the glove compartment in front of her.

"Thanks, Lisa," Jason said, sincerely grateful. "I know how close you and Ben are, and I hate to ask you to hide anything from him."

Lisa's eyes went dead. "Do you?" she asked indifferently. She didn't really know which of Jason's statements she was questioning; but both were completely untrue. Well, okay, *partially* untrue. He did hate asking her to hide things from Ben—but it never put a stop to the asking. Or to his saying stupid things that he'd then have to ask her to forget. To be honest, she *had* forgotten most of them. She usually let whatever Jason was saying wash over her without paying much attention.

As to his knowing how close she was to Ben—well, that was wrong. She *wasn't* close to Ben. Nobody was. Ben didn't allow anyone anywhere near his own personal emotional space. Ben had erected a shield between himself and the rest of the world a long time ago. She had no idea why, and even less interest in knowing why. Ben was a contradiction: he kept everything he thought and felt bottled up, allowing no more than a crack to show, ever. But he acted in any way he pleased, without regard to the consequences. So his actions showed his emotions, she supposed. When she had first met him, that air of perpetual uncertainty was what had thrilled her. Her life before Ben had been routine, boringly, mind-numbingly predictable. Ben had offered her that air of dangerous uncertainty that she had thought she wanted.

And now? Now she knew only that she didn't want that, either. There was a hollow place within her soul that nothing had ever seemed to fill. She knew it was there, but she had no idea *why* it was there, nor how to satisfy it. Her parents' wealth and lifestyle hadn't made an impact on it, and now Ben's casual violence and utter unpredictability hadn't, either. So what would? What was it that she was looking for to make her happy?

And then Ben started back for the car, sauntering as if he hadn't a care in the world. *Probably*, Lisa realized, *he hasn't.* Ben didn't worry. He planned, or he improvised, but he never worried, never showed any uncertainty. Perhaps he never felt any. He clambered into the driver's seat, and pulled the key from his pocket.

"It's show time, boys and girls," he said, starting the engine and gunning the gas.

Lisa suddenly felt sick. There was an odd gleam in Ben's eyes, and a slight smile on his face. She knew with absolute certainty that whatever he had planned was going to hurt somebody somehow. . . .

The general's flat conviction had chilled Steve. *He really believes it,* Steve realized. *That the Zanti could crush us like insects if they wanted to.* But did they want to? What *did* they really want? "Do you really believe that all they want to do is to use our planet as a place of exile for their criminals and misfits?"

"That's what they said," Hart replied.

"But do you *believe* them?" Steve persisted. He realized that he'd put his finger on the festering sore inside the general's mind. Conflicting emotions played across the older man's face for a moment before he finally replied.

"They claim to be incapable of executing their own species, Steve," he said gently. "Now, if you can't bring yourself to destroy a criminal, then you've got to stash him someplace where he can't do you any harm.''

''And that's the key to the whole thing, isn't it?'' asked Hill bitterly. ''Where he won't do *you* any harm. But what about doing *us* harm? Do they have to send their unwanted to another planet? We use prisons and institutions in our own country. Sometimes on islands, yes, but generally in our own communities. We don't send them off to another world!''

''No, we don't, Major,'' agreed Hart calmly. ''But, then, we haven't perfected interstellar travel yet, have we? If we had, maybe things would look a little different to us.''

Steve felt compelled to play the devil's advocate at this point. ''Historically speaking, what you said just isn't true, Major,'' he said. ''Australia was used for decades as a penal colony. The British didn't worry about whether the Aborigines wanted criminals transported there or not. The same went for the West Indies, and even Colonial America. Removing criminals from where they can affect you is a long-standing human tradition.''

''But one which every civilized country has given up long ago,'' Hill argued.

''Only because there's nowhere on Earth left for us to deport people to,'' Hart replied. ''If Mars or Venus were open to us . . .'' He shrugged. ''Maybe the Zanti see this in exactly the same manner.'' He smiled at Steve. ''I'm glad you see it that way, too.''

''I don't,'' Steve contradicted him. ''I'm just drawing an analogy. What *really* bothers me about the whole thing is the issue of security.''

Hart frowned. ''Security in what way?''

''When we build a prison,'' Steve explained, ''then we put guards in it, huge walls around it and prison cells with locks and bars. What have the Zanti done to ensure that their prisoners will *remain* their prisoners, and not interfere with the human race?''

Nodding, Hart gestured toward the curtain again. ''A very good question indeed, Steve. It deserves an equally good answer. Let me show you the battlefield.'' He led the way out of the smaller room and back toward the maps that Steve had glimpsed earlier.

The flat table held a small model, a relief map of the surrounding area. Hart gestured to a small block of green in the center of the model. ''This is us, Morgue, California.''

Steve nodded, starting his tape recorder going and placing it on the edge of the model, where it would record everything for him to consider and use later. ''No danger of tourists wandering in?'' he asked.

Hart actually cracked a grin at that. ''Morgue has never been a tourist spot. Not every ghost town is intrinsically interesting to the camera crowd, Steve. Anyway,'' he added, more soberly, ''here, here, here, here . . .'' His hand flickered across the board, tracing a perimeter of small green markers. ''These are our patrol spots, enclosing a circle, an unbroken limit around the area we agreed that they could use.'' The latter was a rocky outcropping in the middle of the desert, miles away from anything. ''We have permanent bases being readied, but for the moment we have a sentry at each spot. They're all armed and have orders to kill if necessary.'' He looked up, meeting Steve's even gaze. ''That means we're determined to keep strays from stumbling into the Zanti area, accidentally or otherwise.''

''The UFO crowd, you mean?'' asked Steve. ''There's a whole lot of discussion going on in the fringe groups that I'm sure you're aware of. That the government is clamping down security for their own reasons. That this will be another Roswell cover-up, or worse. That this isn't actually the first time the Zanti have visited us, and they're here for contact or retribution or conquest or whatever. Pick your own conspiracy theory.''

Hart's smile was very genuine. ''And all of those reasons you've just cited are precisely why I argued that we needed someone like you, Steve. Someone to record and report on this event. To show that this isn't another military cover-up.'' He waved his hand around his command center. ''That's why you're being allowed to photograph, record and take transcripts of anything that happens here. There'll be no censorship. You can say and use what you like.''

''I know,'' agreed Steve. ''I wouldn't have accepted the job under any other conditions.''

''I know that.'' Hart snorted. ''Oh, it took some in-fighting and a lot of arguments in the Pentagon and the White House. But eventually everyone saw the sense in it. This has to be all open and aboveboard—*after* the fact. Until the Zanti ship touches down, though, there won't be a word about any of this to the media. We don't want to start a panic.'' He gestured back to the board. ''Anyway, as I said, we have armed sentries ringing the entire area. They're not just to keep humans out, though. We're determined to keep the Zanti within. If any of them attempt to leave the designated prison zone, they'll be killed.''

''The Zanti know this?'' asked Steve.

''We've told them,'' Hill broke in, his anger still barely restrained. ''But they have not chosen to respond to that portion of our message.''

Interesting . . . ''And have the Zanti made any arrangements to ensure that their prisoners will not escape?'' Steve wondered.

''If they have,'' Hill replied, ''then they haven't bothered to share it with us. Their only response to that question, and I quote, was: *''That is not your concern.''*

''The blazes it isn't,'' Steve muttered, understanding yet

again more of the reason for Hill's barely contained anger. "The incarceration of who knows how many alien criminals on our world is *not our concern*?"

Hart patted his arm. "Steve, I understand your worry, and to a certain extent I share it. But we all think that the Zanti know what they're talking about. Remember, they're very rigid in their thought processes, and they don't like being questioned."

"A convenient excuse," scoffed Hill.

Ignoring him, Hart concentrated on Steve. "The fact of the matter is that the Zanti have agreed to all of our terms and restrictions, and have accepted the area we've offered them as quite adequate."

Steve knew why he was being favored; Hart had to make the government's case for all of Steve's readers. This was, after all, potentially the biggest story in the world. Almost everyone on the planet would read it or hear about it. Hart had to look good. If Hill objected, Hart could simply order him to be silent. The only reason he hadn't yet done so was that he didn't want Steve to report something along the lines of "any questioning of orders was met only by the threat of court-martial." Later, probably, Hill would get chewed out for being too brutally honest. Still, that wasn't Steve's problem; Hill should understand the military processes by now.

"And suppose they decide *not* to land where we've *offered* to let them land?" Steve asked.

Hart, on solid ground once again, gestured at the model again. "Missile base, here," he said, showing a block of orange color. "We're also in communication with two orbital killsats."

Steve whistled. "Killer satellites? I thought we don't *have* any?"

Hart grinned. "Officially, we didn't. These are holdovers from an earlier time, called back on line just in case. We've had a flight trajectory filed from the Zanti. If their penal ship is more than ten degrees off target, we destroy it, instantly. As I said, the Zanti know this, and have agreed.''

''Which all comes back to the question of whether or not we can actually track their ship,'' Steve pointed out. ''After all, if they *do* have stealth technology, then the ship could come down anywhere, and we'd not know about it until afterward.''

''If the Zanti intended to betray our trust like that,'' Hart argued, ''then why all of this elaborate setup? No, Steve, I'm certain you're just allowing paranoia to get the better of you here.''

Steve smiled. ''Just asking the necessary questions, General,'' he murmured. ''If I don't, you can be sure there are millions of people outside that cordon of yours who will ask them.''

''Of course.'' Hart gestured back to the map again. ''We're also equipped to destroy the ship *after* it's landed, should that prove necessary. That entire area has been mined. If there's the slightest suspicion that the Zanti criminals will escape, then we can detonate the whole mesa if we have to in order to prevent such an occurrence. Trust me, Steve, we've thought of everything.''

''Let's hope so,'' Steve agreed. There was still a sick feeling of fear inside him. Despite all the general's assurances, and all the precautions, he couldn't help feeling that it would all be inadequate if the Zanti weren't being honest with the human race.

And he was a professor of communications. A very young one, admittedly, but one all the same. His entire career had been spent studying communications in every shape and form known to man. And his intuition told him with absolute certainly one very clear fact: the Zanti were somehow lying.

He couldn't pinpoint it. It might simply be a lie by omission—neglecting deliberately to let the humans in on some crucial piece of information. Or it could be a deliberate lie, a falsehood told to appease the lesser species until the aims of the Zanti were accomplished and it was too late for the humans to object or respond. Either way, he'd stake his career on the fact that there was something being hidden from them. Since they seemed to have some time to go yet, maybe he could spend it studying the transcripts of the Zanti conversations with the military. If there was some area that was being carefully avoided, maybe he could spot it. At any rate, it would give him something to do while he was waiting, apart from bothering the poor technicians with his inane questions about their jobs and what they aimed to do.

"General Hart?" a voice called out, cutting across the low-level noise of the room. Hart spun around, instantly alert, his affable pose evaporating and the stern features and demeanor of the professional soldier replacing them. The man was manning one of the consoles for which Steve as yet had no name. He wore a thin headset, now pushed back slightly. "It's the Zanti ship," he said. "Communication has been established."

Hart nodded, and marched briskly across the room. Steve snatched up his cassette recorder hastily, prepared to follow. There was a slight tug on his arm, and he turned to see the troubled face of Major Hill.

"Now it begins," Hill said softly. "But how will it end?"

Steve nodded his agreement. Indeed, how would all of this end? With an anticlimax? Or with a bang that might signal the end of the human race? There was only one way to find out, and he followed General Hart to where the Zanti awaited them.

CHAPTER 5

THE TECHNICIAN HANDED General Hart a headset, which he slipped on and then carefully adjusted. He glanced down at the soldier, who nodded slightly and then tapped commands on his panel.

Steve's throat went dry. He'd seen transcripts of most of the Zanti messages, but he'd never actually heard one. What would these alien beings sound like? Would he be able to gather any understanding of their minds from the inflections in their voices? Or would it be sealed off from him across an unbridgeable gulf between the human and the alien? Did mankind and the Zanti have any common reference points at all?

Glancing around the room, he realized that the buzz of work had virtually stopped. Everyone there was focused on the general and the speakers. Steve could feel the tension and uncertainty. He wasn't the only one here wondering what would happen next: they all were.

"This is General Maximilian R. Hart," the general said,

his voice firm and strong, "of the Strategic Air Command, United States Air Force." There was barely a pause, and he added, "Of the planet Earth."

That's exactly it, thought Steve. For once, the human race was working as one. Faced with the outsider, people could all pull together. The Zanti landing wasn't taking place so much on *American* soil as on *human* soil.

"Come in, please," Hart concluded. He nodded at the technician, who tapped controls.

"Signal sent and received," he reported. He scanned his panel. "They're getting the message," he confirmed. "No reply."

The pause lasted several seconds, and then Hart spoke into the microphone again. "Zanti penal ship, come in, please."

There was still nothing. The speakers hummed slightly with background noise, but there was no message. Steve glanced around the room again. Everyone was frozen into place, barely even breathing as they awaited the reply that didn't seem to be coming. Had something gone wrong?

The thought must have occurred to Hart as well. He turned to the radar operator. "They couldn't have landed already, could they?" he demanded.

The young soldier shook his head, but rechecked his instruments. "Our screens would have shown it," he said with absolute confidence in his equipment. "There's no signal from the ground stations, sir, and nothing from the satellites, either. There's nothing showing."

"Unless they have stealth capacities," Hill murmured into Steve's ear, echoing his own grim thoughts. "In which case they could be anywhere at all and we'd be none the wiser."

Either Hart didn't hear this comment or else he simply decided to ignore it. He nodded to the communications operator and tried once more. "Zanti penal ship, this is General Maximilian R. Hart of the Strategic Air Command. I am the same man who concluded negotiations with your government commander on our time pattern described in your records as SE six-six-zero.'' He paused for a moment before plunging on: ''We have cleared the area guaranteed to you on that date. You may expect to land without interference and without incident. I repeat, it is safe for you to land. Please communicate.''

He finished, and then stared at the speakers, waiting to see if this time there would be a reply. Steve's eyes were drawn to them as well, as he wondered what the problem was. Were the Zanti simply not interested in talking anymore? Had they said all that they wanted in past communications? Or were they concerned about Hart's credentials? Were they checking that they were speaking to the appropriate person? They did seem overly keen on due process and a rigidly defined hierarchy. Maybe they would only speak to the top man? Or—

There was a sudden change in the intensity of the background hiss from the speakers. It became somehow tinny, almost grating.

And then came the voice.

Steve was recording it as he listened. The voice was flat, emotionless and utterly inhuman. It spoke without pause, without any stress on the words. The voice itself was high-pitched, but with an almost nasal drone to it, and a curious low tone underlying it. It sounded as if it were actually being produced by two very different voice boxes at one time. The tone was harsh and grating, like fingers on a chalkboard. Steve winced, his skin crawling as he listened to what was said.

''Zeen faq I lanz trinsini ob krel ob a mang sil lanz prad o veen o sil lanz,'' it said, all in a single breath. It spoke for about fifteen more seconds, each syllable distinct and yet quite clearly some alien tongue. Steve could make nothing of it. Then the signal stopped.

Hart nodded to the technician. ''Translation,'' he ordered.

The man had been taping the message, and he now nodded at the woman at the console next to his. She tapped commands into her keyboard, and the computer murmured to itself for a few seconds. Then the speakers sprang to life once again.

Steve was thankful that the computer had taken some of the grating harshness out of the Zanti's voice. It still didn't sound quite human, but at least this time it didn't make Steve's skin prickle.

"This is First Regent of Penal Ship One," the Zanti said. "We are ready to land in designated area. We have reason to suspect your good faith. Landing area surrounded. Weapons threateningly angled."

Hill leaned forward again. "Penal Ship *One*," he repeated softly. "How many others are there? The agreement was supposed to be for only the one, containing their worst misfits. Are they planning on following it up later with more?"

That was something Steve obviously couldn't answer. He realized that Hill was simply sharing his own fears. It was obvious that the major was having a paranoia attack. And, Steve reflected, probably not without reason.

Hart spoke again. "We have no other way of keeping the area clear for you," he said, trying to sound as sincere as possible. "Our roads and deserts are generally open to all men. The sentries are there only to guard your privacy."

Would the Zanti accept that? Steve rubbed at the back of his neck, trying to relieve some of the tension that racked his body. Hart was lying, of course: the sentries and missiles were there as a two-edged sword, capable of striking human intruders—or Zanti treachery. Would the Zanti understand that? And if they did, would they find it acceptable?

The grating voice began again. "Ple bien zo a lanz tri ob trinsini," it said. "Lanz trinsini lobo zan a mang lis lanz ob." Steve tried to shut his ears to the worst of its effects, but he was still repulsed by the tone of it. If the Zanti voices affected him this badly, how would he react to the aliens themselves?

Assuming, of course, that he ever got to see any.

The translator chirped to itself, and then the speakers came to life again: "We shall land," the Zanti announced. "Our privacy must be maintained. Total destruction to anyone who invades it." There was a click, clearly signaling the end of the transmission.

Steve shook his head. It didn't sound like *anyone* was going to get to meet the Zanti. Hart was correct: they were really paranoid about their privacy. "Total destruction to anyone who invades it," he repeated to himself. No compromise in that. Swift, certain retaliation. What kind of beings were these Zanti?

The general heard his comment, and managed a thin smile. "Don't worry, Steve," he said. "The only way anyone would get near that ship when it lands is over someone's dead body."

Somehow, that didn't make Steve feel any better at all.

Lisa could feel the sweat trickling down her back as the car came out of the shade of the mine and into the bright sunlight again. The air in the car almost instantly became stifling, and she clicked on the air-conditioning, immediately turning it up high. This would not be the best day to try to cross the desert, but they had no option.

Ben was humming to himself as he floored the accelerator pedal. The car howled as it sprang forward. Twenty, thirty, forty . . . The speed rose as the car surged up the hill toward the shack. There was a smile in his eyes and one frozen very slightly on his face, and Lisa was suddenly aware that there was something very wrong going on. Ben was never this happy unless he was planning on hurting someone.

And then she saw everything with utter clarity, but without being able to do anything at all about it. It was like one of those dreams where you try to escape from some menace, but you're moving too slowly to be able to get anywhere. Straight ahead of them, she saw the guard, carrying a case of supplies toward the cabin from the stockpile the truck had left. Ben was guiding the car directly toward the man.

The soldier dropped his case, and slipped the weapon from his shoulder, raising it and opening fire.

For a second, the world seemed to whirl dizzily about her. Lisa realized that the soldier wasn't simply trying to stop them—he was trying to kill them. And Ben was trying to kill *him*. She heard two screaming voices, knowing rather abstractly that one was hers and one Jason's. She heard the sound of bullets *ching*ing against the side of the Thunderbird, and then—

Impact.

The force of the blow slowed the car for a second as it slammed into the soldier's body. Lisa clearly saw his face for a brief second, the horror written on it. *He's barely older than I am*, she thought in wonder and sick terror. *Just a kid who joined the army to see the world. And all he's seen is a desert and his own death.*

Then the body snapped forward, rolling across the hood of the car, as Ben gunned the gas again. For another brief second, the dead soldier's face seemed to stare through the windshield at Lisa, his open mouth and lifeless eyes an accusation against her. The butt of his rifle cracked against the glass, sending a thread of cracks across the lower portion of the windshield. Then momentum carried the body over the edge of the car and hurled it at the hard desert floor to one side.

She could see the battered, broken body in the rearview mirror. There was surprisingly little blood. She'd expected a huge pool of it over everything, including the car, but there were just two small streaks of red in the dust on the hood.

Then realization hit her with its full force. Ben had deliberately killed the soldier, to stop him from stopping them. She had just been a witness to a cold-blooded murder.

No, not a witness. A *participant*. She was an accessory. If the police caught up with them now, she'd be tried for murder.

Two dead eyes stared back at her. *That's exactly what you are*, they seemed to accuse her. *Murderer!*

She felt sick, unclean and ready to throw up. From the sound of things in the back, Jason had beaten her to it on all three points.

Beside her, Ben started to whistle rather tunelessly as he steered the car through the desert rocks, and off toward the Nevada state line. He didn't seem to be bothered by what he had done at all. On the contrary, she realized, he'd *enjoyed* himself. Like with the bank teller, she understood. It was all a matter of power with Ben, as so many things in his life were. He didn't want money, or girls, or success. He wanted the power of life and death, the ability to choose who would live and whom he would kill. It was the one thing that gave his life meaning. A terrible, bleak and evil meaning. And she was stuck with him, like it or loathe it.

She tried to focus her mind, to wipe out the face of the dead soldier from her thoughts, to concentrate only on the desert road ahead of them. It was an impossible task. What had she managed to get herself into now? And what would happen next? The army wasn't going to let them get away with what they had done. She realized the Thunderbird was leaving tracks in the road that anyone could follow. How long would it be before the military came after them?

And then what?

What had Ben managed to get them into now? Lisa had a strong feeling that this was going to be a day that she'd never be able to erase from her nightmares.

She had no idea just how right this premonition would turn out to be. . . .

CHAPTER 6

WE'RE PICKING UP a signal from the satellites, sir," the tracking operator announced. "They're coming in."

Steve leaned forward, and saw the pulsing light on the scanner that indicated the path of the incoming Zanti ship. Excitement was starting to bubble through the room as the culmination of their efforts drew closer. The murmur of voices started up again, and people started to move about, seeing to their duties as finally something was happening.

"Is it on track?" Hart demanded immediately.

"Yes, sir," the technician replied. "Within three degrees of specified parameters."

"Good." Hart nodded once. "Keep on it, and let me know if anything changes at all." He spun around, and managed a smile for Steve. "So far, everything looks fine. What did you think of the contact?"

"They seemed . . . very abrupt," Steve answered thoughtfully. "It sounds almost like they're nervous to me."

"Probably they are," the general answered. "After all, this is the first time that they've done anything like this."

"So they say," Hill couldn't resist commenting.

Hart gave him an icy glare. "We have no reason to doubt their word, Major," he snapped.

"And no good reason to believe it, either, sir," Hill answered.

"They're keeping to the agreement so far," Hart pointed out. "That at least is good news. And if—" He broke off as a telephone rang. He turned to look at the red emergency line, which was throbbing.

"Trouble?" asked Steve quickly.

"No, not necessarily," Hart replied. He strode to the phone; everyone else in the room was staring at it, but none of them seemed to be authorized to answer it. Hart scooped it up. "Yes, sir, Mr. President? General Hart speaking."

The presidential hot line . . . Steve realized that the president had to have his own staff monitoring everything. He'd no doubt heard the same exchange between Hart and the Zanti that Steve had, and was now checking firsthand. There had to be a great deal of tension in Washington over this affair.

"No," Hart said quietly. "No apprehension in this area."

That's not quite true, Steve realized, sneaking a glimpse at Hill. The major's face was moist with sweat, and he was wiping his palms on the legs of his trousers. *Hill is very apprehensive indeed. And perhaps with good reason. He's right: there's no real reason to trust the Zanti yet.* Hart believed the Zanti were nervous because this was the first time they'd ever done anything like this. But it was possible that they were nervous simply because they were lying to the humans, and were worried about the outcome. *Face it*, Steve realized, *everyone involved in this matter is apprehensive. Especially me.*

"Well, you heard the contact tape, sir," Hart was saying.

"It sounds to me like they're more worried about us than we are about them."

That's debatable, Steve knew. But the general had to put the most positive spin on matters that he could. Steve understood that. He could only hope Hart wasn't being tremendously naive.

"It should be landing within a quarter of an hour," Hart commented. "They're already on the fringes of our atmosphere, and right on the correct path. The way we're organized here, sir, we'll be able to recognize any hostile intentions within the first five minutes of landing. We're on full alert, and the missile bases are standing by. I recommend that you remain monitoring events as they occur." He paused a moment and then nodded. "Fine. Thank you, sir." He handed the phone to the nearest technician. "Monitor this line," he ordered. "It stays open. If the White House squeaks, yell for me, no matter what's happening."

"Yes, sir!" The technician grabbed the phone, and started to work on his console to monitor the line. Hart turned away, and gestured for Steve to join him. As Steve moved to do so, another technician glanced up from his panel.

"Sir!" he called. "Tracking stations are starting to pick up the Zanti ship. Two radio telescope facilities have reported it. It won't be very long before it's visible, and people start calling the TV stations and newspapers."

Hart nodded. "There's nothing much we can do about it," he said. To Steve, he added; "Come on, Steve. There's something I have to do, and it might interest you." He led the way from the room back to the guard post at the entrance. Steve noticed that Major Hill was following them. The guard opened the outer door with a crisp salute, and Hart led the small party outside, and back into the heat.

The general leaned on the porch railing, and stared up at the sky. Hill moved to join him, and Steve saw that he'd brought a pair of binoculars with him. He used them to scan the sky for a moment, and then handed them wordlessly to the general. Hart examined the same patch of sky, and then held the binoculars out to Steve.

"I always like to see things with my own eyes," he commented. "Makes it that much more personal. You can take a look if you like, Steve."

There was no way he'd turn down an offer like that. Taking the glasses, Steve trained them on the patch of sky the others had been observing. For a moment he saw nothing, and he moved the glasses slightly. A flash of light caught his attention, and he zeroed in on it.

It was pretty disappointing, to be honest. Despite the thrill of knowing that he was looking at a spaceship from an alien world, it was still too high up to make anything out. It was just a glint of silver in the sky, a thin contrail lagging behind it. It was impossible to make out any details at all. He hoped this wasn't the only chance he'd get to see the ship. To be sitting almost on top of it when it landed and yet to see nothing . . . It would be incredibly frustrating. And yet the Zanti had made their demand for complete privacy more than clear.

"Steve?" Hart asked, holding out his hand. Steve passed him the binoculars, lost in thought as the general scanned the sky again.

"I wonder if we're going to get to see one of them," Steve mused. What would they be like? He couldn't forget the revulsion he'd felt at hearing the Zanti voice. Would he have the same experience if he was allowed to see one of the Zanti? Or would they be beautiful? Or maybe simply . . . different? It would be exciting to find out.

"Perhaps more than one," Hill commented. He leaned against one of the upright posts, looking up at the sky. "If they're anything at all like Earth men, they aren't going to like being cooped up in a prison ship any more than we like being locked up behind bars.'' He glanced at Hart and then at Steve. ''I believe they'll try to break free.''

Hart spun around, an angry expression on his face. ''That's enough of that kind of talk,'' he snapped. ''The Zanti commander guaranteed maximum control of the prisoners. They will be guarded constantly.''

Refusing to back down, Hill replied quietly, ''Every prison guarantees maximum control of its prisoners. Despite that, men still manage to break out. Can we afford to believe that the Zanti are any less resourceful than our human prisoners?''

It was a good question, Steve knew. And one to which there really was no answer but faith. Hart believed the Zanti were telling the truth, so he accepted their assurances. Hill believed they were lying, so he questioned everything they said. Steve wasn't yet certain which side he stood on, except that he believed that the Zanti were hiding something.

''Do we have any idea what these misfits have done?'' he asked, attempting to break the tension between the two officers. ''I mean, are they the Zanti equivalent of murderers—or just folks who didn't pay their parking tickets?''

He'd been hoping for a slight smile at his joke, but he was disappointed. Hart shook his head. ''The Zanti haven't told us anything outside the fact that these prisoners are unable to fit into their society in the correct fashion.''

''In other words,'' Hill completed, ''they could be anything from political prisoners being exiled for believing in the wrong causes up to mass murderers. And they're going to be in our backyard.''

It was a sobering thought. If Hill was right and some of the Zanti escaped, would they apply for political asylum—or go on a murderous rampage?

The door behind them opened, and the guard came out. Steve glanced up, and then stiffened. The man was pale and almost shaking.

Something had gone wrong. . . .

"General," the guard gasped, managing a shaky salute. "We've picked up something on ground radar," he reported. "It's inside the periphery. We think it's an automobile."

Steve didn't need to see the shock in Hart's face, because he knew it was on his own. The Zanti had demanded complete privacy—at the threat of death. And now it looked as if Hart's defenses had been breached. If the report was true, this could be the start of the end of the human race. . . .

Hart pushed past the guard, rushing back inside his command post. Hill and Steve were only a second behind him.

Disaster . . .

In the desert, the car ground to a halt, its engine spluttering and then dying. Ben cursed and slammed his hand on the wheel in frustration. Scowling, he glanced at the gas indicator, which was on zero. "It can't be," he muttered. Then, as a thought struck him, he opened the door and glanced backward. "The gas tank's been punctured," he said softly. "One of the sentry's shots must have hit it."

Lisa shuddered at the thought. "We were lucky the car didn't explode." She had the mental picture of a fireball enveloping her, and she couldn't stop shaking.

"That kind of nonsense only happens in movies," Ben replied. He closed the door again and stared out of the windshield. "We won't be driving any further now."

Jason leaned on the back of Lisa's seat, licking at his lips. "Then they're going to catch us, aren't they, Ben? We just have to sit here and wait for them to catch up with us."

"Shut up," Ben said softly. He was obviously thinking, calculating the angles he could play. After a moment, he lowered his window.

"Close the window, Ben," Lisa said gently. She could almost feel the heat already, soaking into the car.

"With the engine dead, the air conditioner isn't working," Ben pointed out.

Lisa didn't care. "Close the window, Ben." She wanted to be isolated from the open spaces outside the car. She wanted to hide within herself, to try to pretend that none of this was happening. She kept seeing the poor man's face as he hit the windshield. It wouldn't go away. She found herself starting to shake again, and clamped her right hand around her left wrist, willing herself to stop.

Ben noticed it, of course. Ben noticed everything. "I'm going to tell you something," he said, softly but urgently. "You probably won't believe it, but it's true. I would never hurt a reasonable man."

"Open the window, Ben," Lisa answered. "You're choking the air with your stinking lies."

Ben scowled. He didn't like to be disbelieved. "That soldier opened fire on us. He didn't give us any warning, any chance to stop."

"It may have been his orders to do that," Lisa said. "He may have been told to stop intruders at whatever cost." *Besides*, she thought to herself, *you aimed the car at him before you even knew that. You were always intending to kill him.* As always, Ben was trying to make himself look like he had no option but to do whatever he had already decided to do. He loved to justify everything he did. He wanted her to agree with him that it had been necessary. Like he did whenever he hit her. He always had a perfectly good reason, he would insist, and he would demand that she agree with him. She invariably did, knowing that he'd only get more violent if she didn't. But right now she didn't care what Ben did. She wasn't going to give him the satisfaction of pretending she was on his side this time.

"We can't afford to be captured, Lisa," Ben said, changing tack slightly. "None of us. I'm a three-time loser. If I'm caught, it'll be life for me—at best. Jason too, most likely. Right, Jase?''

The youth nodded, his face twisted in fear. ''Right. I've been inside twice already. This time, they'll throw the book at me for sure.'' He screwed his eyes closed, trying to cut off all sight of the real world, retreating to his own private mental hell.

''And what about you, Lisa?'' Ben asked. ''Do you think you could go back? Even all your daddy's money couldn't buy you out of jail time for all of this.''

Lisa sighed. ''My friends—what few I had—all asked me why I was going away with you. 'He's a psychopath and he's not good looking.' They were the nicest things anyone said about you. And I told them I was going with you because you were not safe and sane and secure.'' She shook her head slightly. ''My parents always kept me safe and sane and secure, and I was *dying* from it. I couldn't take it anymore. I like adventure, Ben. Bad adventure, even, but just so that *something* would happen. I couldn't take the boredom anymore. And I knew that, whatever else you might be, you would never be boring.''

He smiled at this, taking it all as a compliment. Which, she supposed, it was meant to be. She had wanted adventure, anything to kill the dullness of her life. Well, her life certainly wasn't dull now. But it was potentially deadly. ''I know my need will destroy me someday,'' she added. ''But I can't help it.'' She stared out of the window at the desert. ''Can't you do anything about the car?''

Ben shrugged. ''It needs gas. And there's no station for a hundred miles.'' He reached for the glove compartment, opening it up. Inside was a small flask filled with water. As he pulled it out, several of the bundles of twenties fell to the carpet. Lisa glanced over her shoulder, and saw Jason's eyes open wide. He started to reach forward, then thought better of it. Ben took a swig of water and recapped the flask. He didn't offer it to either of the others. Lisa hadn't expected him to do so. Ben never shared unless he was making a point. He pushed it back into the glove compartment. "Pick up the money," he ordered.

Lisa didn't move. She wasn't interested in the money; she never had been. The robberies had never been about money for her. They were about excitement. Only Jason and Ben had cared about the take. Money, to her, was something she wished she'd never have to touch again in her life. It repelled her.

"Pick up the money," Ben repeated, an edge to his voice.

Suddenly, she could take it no longer. All the events of the past few weeks bubbled up inside her, threatening to overwhelm her sanity. The robberies, the running, the hiding, the death of that poor guard . . . Lisa wanted to scream. Instead, she opened her door and started to climb out.

Ben's hand fastened on her arm. It was a painful hold, but she refused to let it show on her face. "There's no place to go, Lisa," he said softly.

"Yes there is," she answered, not looking at him. "I'm going back to the shack. When the army comes to investigate, I'm going to give myself up. Maybe facing up to what I've done will be the biggest adventure of my life." She jerked her hand free, and climbed out of the car, directly into the throbbing, heat-filled air.

Ben slid across after her. As she stood there, momentarily stunned by the heat rising from the parched earth, he clambered out beside her. He kicked a bundle of money from the car as he did so. Wordlessly, he simply stood there.

Shielding her eyes against the sun, Lisa started to walk back the way they had driven. This was probably a very foolish idea, she knew, but she had simply reached her limit. All the attraction that Ben had held for her had evaporated faster than water in this desert heat.

"Lisa," Ben called softly.

Lisa recognized that tone. Ben was always quietest when he was being dangerous. Slowly, she turned to stare back at him.

He was leaning against the car, casually. "Come here," he said. "Come here."

There was no use in pretending. She knew when she was defeated. Slowly, she retraced her steps to the car. Ben had a blank expression on his face, showing no anger or emotion at all. She knew from experience that this meant he might erupt into violence at any second.

"Now pick up the money," he ordered.

Lisa bent to do so, and then she collected the other bills that were still inside the car. She avoided meeting Jason's wide-eyed look of embarrassed shock, and instead stuffed the money back into the glove compartment and slammed it shut.

"You know you can't give yourself up, Lisa," Ben said, gently and rationally. "If you did, the police would make you tell them everything. You know you can't hold out against pressure, Lisa. You crumble. You'd be forced to tell them all about me. And then the police would put me away forever. And I can't allow that. You know I can't." He stared off into the desert, as if something had caught his attention.

Lisa frowned, and then she identified it. It was a low noise that she'd been hearing since she left the car but hadn't really paid any attention to. A rhythmic beeping sound, coming from the air in the direction of a large stack of rocks several hundred yards away. It was like nothing she'd ever heard before, and she simply couldn't place it. It had obviously caught Ben's attention for some reason.

She had no idea what it could be. What would anything be doing out here in the desert? She could think of nothing that would make any sense. But, whatever it was, it must have something to do with that dead army guard.

What was going on here? What had they stumbled into?

The noise was getting slowly louder and louder, as if something was flying toward them. . . .

CHAPTER 7

BEN, SHIELDING HIS eyes from the sun, was scanning the skies, looking for the source of the noise. He looked ready to go off to investigate it. Lisa suddenly didn't want him to go.

"People die in the desert," she informed him.

He didn't look around. "Are you afraid to die?"

Lisa didn't know the answer to that one. Yes, the thought of dying scared her. But so did the thought of living, either the life she had right now with Ben, or even returning to her old life with her parents. Either way, death might be preferable. But if she said so, she knew that there was a very good chance that Ben might resolve her dilemma by using his gun on her. And, tired and drained as she was, she wasn't ready for that yet. "Suppose I tell the police that *I* stole the money?" she suggested, changing the subject. "There's no need to even mention you."

Ben smiled slightly, and straightened up a little. In his best

Joe Friday impression, he asked her, "Why did you have to steal the money, Ms. Lawrence? Don't your wealthy parents give you everything that you need? Just the facts, ma'am."

Lisa couldn't help herself; she laughed at his silly impression. "Three-time losers are supposed to be the most desperate people in all the world," she commented. "But not you, Ben. You never seem to feel desperation. You just rub that magic lamp of your imagination for inspiration, and you seem to escape all fear and pain. Nothing gets you down for long, does it?"

Ben was still having fun playing detective. "Well, the whole town knows that your parents wouldn't let you go to the mall on your own and spend a dime. They had to be with you, to help you buy anything. So maybe that's why you stole the money, so you could shop till you dropped without your parents staring over your shoulder and helping you to pick what was just right for your sweet little image. But tell me, girlie, whatever made you shoot the teller? And why did you run down that armed guard out there in the desert? You killed him, you know."

The casual, joking way he talked about the murder made Lisa shiver. There was nothing she could think of to answer that mocking question. She turned away from his piercing gaze, and Ben laughed.

"Not quite up to it, are you, Lisa?" he asked in his normal voice. "Taking the rap for assault, manslaughter and murder isn't quite what you had in mind, is it? You might think you could take being locked up for a few months for robbery, but how about spending the rest of your life in prison for murder, huh?" He grinned at her again. "It'd be like being home again, with someone dictating every last move you make. Only without all the rich furnishings that might make such a hell bearable. No nice clothes, no fancy foods, no servants to wait on you. Just a thin prison dress, barely edible food and a small cell to call your own. Do you *really* think that you could go back to that?''

Defeat lay in her stomach like a rock. Ben was right: she'd sooner be dead than imprisoned forever. ''I never could stand too much sun,'' she muttered, and clambered back into the car. She pulled the door shut, feeling very weak and wretched.

Laughing, Ben started to move around to his side of the car. Then he stopped and looked up again, shielding his eyes from the glare. ''Lisa, Jason!'' he called. ''Come out here!''

With a sigh, Lisa climbed out again. She was beyond questioning any of his orders now. Jason scrambled out to join them in the sun.

''What do you suppose that is?'' Ben asked her, pointing upward.

Lisa squinted at the sky, her hand shielding her eyes. At first she couldn't see anything, and then she caught a glimpse of silver, gleaming in the sunlight. A plane? Did the military have a plane or a helicopter out looking for them? But . . . the shape was all wrong. There was no sign of any wings or a tail or anything. It looked like it was perfectly round, and as far as she knew, the military had nothing like that flying. . . .

Unless this was one of those top-secret bases she'd heard about, where they were developing some stealth bomber or something. Or maybe even that Area 51, where there was supposed to be a crashed flying saucer that the Air Force was trying to rebuild and get flying again.

Whatever it was up there in the sky, Lisa knew that it spelled trouble for them. Because it was obviously what was being guarded by the soldiers. They shouldn't be seeing this. And now that they had? She glanced at Jason, who was standing in shock and bewilderment, and then at Ben. For once, she saw that his mask of indifference was gone. He was completely puzzled—and intrigued.

Whatever they were seeing, he wanted to know more. Lisa

understood that this would only cause further trouble, but she also knew that it would be fruitless to argue with Ben once he'd made up his mind. She was certain that nothing but bad would come from any of this. And that there was nothing she could possibly do to prevent it.

Inside the forward command base, there was an air of barely restrained panic at the news of the intruder. Hart was thunderstruck for a moment, and then he snapped into action.

"Establish a red alert at the missile base," he snapped at the communications technician. Then he spun around to one of the women. "Get onto every sentry post immediately," he ordered. "I want to know how *anything* bigger than a gnat got past any one of them. I'm going to have someone's hide for this." To the radio technician, he said, "Get me the Zanti ship on the line immediately, if not sooner." To another man: "I want everything ground radar can tell me about the vehicle. Move!"

They moved.

That was one good thing about the military, Steve knew: once orders had been given, everyone rushed to obey them with the maximum of effort and minimum of fuss. He glanced at Hill, who was leaning over the radar screen. "How bad is it?" he asked.

Hill straightened and shrugged. "There's no way it can be considered good," he answered. "The Zanti have insisted time after time on being left alone." He gestured at the ground radar screen. "They're bound to see this as a breach of good faith. The only question is how seriously they'll take it. Will they call off their ship? Or will they just bomb us all to dust? Take an educated guess, because there's nothing better open to us right now. You may just have a ringside seat for the first real war of the worlds, Grave." He turned back to the screen.

Steve knew that Hill was right: there was absolutely no predicting what was going to happen next. Well, he'd come here to cover this event, expecting it to be historical. Now it might even be the end of human history, if the Zanti felt betrayed. Various emotions raged within him—fear, panic, exhilaration and professional curiosity. The latter finally won out, though it was a close call. He knew that it wouldn't take much to push him over the edge into the panic that lay just beneath his professional surface. He moved closer to where General Hart was awaiting some answers.

The first came from the woman checking the sentries. "Post nine is not responding, sir," she reported. "That's Corporal Delano. I'm having a jeep investigate right now."

Hart nodded his approval, and continued to wait, ignoring the frenzied activity around him. Steve caught his eyes straying toward the red hot line, but he made no move for it. The president must know by now what was happening here. If he wanted an update, Hart clearly wanted to have all the facts at hand before calling in.

Two minutes later, the female technician spoke up again. "The patrol reports that Corporal Delano is dead, sir. He's been struck by a moving vehicle."

Hart nodded. "Which way was the vehicle headed?"

"Into the Zanti landing area," she replied.

"That explains it," Hart commented.

Steve frowned. "You think somebody found out about the ship and deliberately crashed the guard post?"

"Maybe," Hart replied. "Maybe it's something else. Either way, we're in serious trouble because of it."

"Are you going to search for the car?" asked Steve.

"We can't," Hart said bitterly. "It's in the Zanti landing area. One vehicle in there is a breach of our understanding with the Zanti. If I were to send in more to search for that first one, the Zanti are bound to see that as betrayal. I can't afford it." He sighed. "We're just going to have to wait and see what happens next."

The communications technician called out, "Sir, the Zanti are definitely receiving our signals. But they're not responding."

Hart shook his head. "Maybe they're too busy with the flight details." He glanced at the radar technician. "How are they doing?"

The technician studied his screen. "They're just about down now, sir, and right on target. They're landing."

Grave knew that they had now come to the crux of the entire mission: the Zanti had finally arrived.

What would happen next?

"Something weird's going on around here, Lisa," said Ben softly. His eyes were alive with curiosity. "That sentry. The army. That whatever-it-was we just saw and heard. Something's happening around here, and I want to know what it is."

"I don't," Jason said, fear quite evident in his voice. "I just want to get away from here." Both Lisa and Ben completely ignored him.

"Let's wait in the car, Ben," Lisa suggested.

"Wait?" Ben blinked, puzzled. "For what?"

"Until they find us," Lisa answered.

Ben snorted. "The police? The army?"

"Whoever."

He shook his head, and then gestured toward the rocks ahead of them. "Whatever that thing was, it came down there somewhere. Aren't you at all curious about it?"

"What thing, Ben?" asked Lisa, deliberately keeping any emotion out of her voice. He was playing a game again. This time it was explorer, or big game hunter, or something. It was how he avoided reality, by recasting himself time and time again in different roles. She wasn't going to encourage him anymore.

"It looked like some kind of spaceship." Ben laughed delightedly. "Don't you think it looked like a spaceship?"

Yes, Lisa thought, but she'd never say it aloud. It scared her too much to even start to think about what it might have been.

"You got chills?" he asked her suddenly.

"Chills?" she answered blankly. Abruptly, she realized she was indeed shivering. "Yes," she murmured. She knew that it had to be over a hundred degrees out in the sun, but she couldn't stop shivering.

"It's just fear," Ben said casually. He took her elbow, amused at her goose bumps, and led her back to the car.

"I suppose so," agreed Lisa, knowing it was true. She was absolutely terrified. Not just of the sight she'd seen, but of everything that had happened to her today. It was way too much for her to handle. She sat down in the car. Jason scuttled into the back seat again.

"Shock," Ben said with authority. He was holding on to the door, looking thoughtful, as if fear wasn't an emotion he'd ever felt, and he couldn't really understand it. For all Lisa knew, that was exactly how he felt.

"I want to close the door, Ben," she said, shaking. Inside the car, with the doors closed, she'd feel safer. Maybe not a lot safer, but she'd take whatever she could get.

Ben smiled at her abruptly. "*You* think I'm good-looking, don't you?" he asked her, still holding on to the door.

For a moment, Lisa had no idea what he was talking about. Then she recalled their earlier conversation. "No, Ben," she said honestly. She didn't care how he'd take the news.

He just shrugged. "Just not dull?" he asked.

"Just not dull," she agreed. "Never that."

Letting go of the door, he said, "Close the door, Lisa." He

turned and started to walk away, toward the rocks.

"Ben," Lisa called softly.

He stopped and looked back over his shoulder, his twisted grin lighting his face. "I'll be right back," he promised. "I just want to go and look at that spaceship." He flicked his fingers in her direction, and resumed his steady walk.

Lisa closed the door, and sat there for a moment, her mind blank. She'd even forgotten that Jason was still with her until he spoke up, quite close to her ear.

"Why do you let him treat you like that?" he asked her. "I wouldn't ever treat a girl of mine like that."

"You don't have a girl, Jason," Lisa pointed out, refusing to open her eyes. Maybe she could will everything to just go away and leave her in peace.

"No, but if I did, I'd treat her real nice," he answered. She could hear the scowl in his voice. "I'd buy her things, take her places. Treat her real nice."

"I'm sure you would," Lisa agreed. "With all the money you steal, you could show a girl a really good time. Until you got caught."

That made him pause for a moment, but not for long. Lisa realized he was talking for the same reason she was shaking: out of fear. He needed conversation, reasurrance. Well, she supposed she could at least supply the conversation.

"Why do you stick with him?" he asked.

Lisa snorted. "Because if I tried to leave him, he'd probably kill me, Jason. And I'm not ready to die. Not just yet, at least. I still want to live. Though sometimes I wonder what I want to live *for*."

"You didn't say you stick with him because you love him," Jason said. He sounded vaguely satisfied with that point. Was he developing a crush on her? It was possible, she supposed. It was also likely to get him killed if Ben ever found out.

"Love?" she repeated, and shook her head. She turned around and opened her eyes to look at him. "Love is just a word that people use, Jason. When my father used it, he'd say, 'You can't do that; I love you and won't allow it.' What he meant by love was *control*. And sometimes Ben will tell me he loves me. Usually right before he hits me. Ben means *control*, too, only in a different way. Neither of them means *love*. It's a hollow word that people fill up with whatever meaning they want."

Jason shook his head. "What about you, Lisa?" he demanded. "Don't you love anyone or anything?"

She considered the question seriously for a moment. "No," she finally decided. "I don't. Not even myself. Because if I did, I'd have left Ben a long time back. I don't love anything or anyone. Maybe that's why there's a hollow in my soul, Jason. One that needs to be filled up with something. Only I don't have a clue as to what that something might be. I was looking to find it in Ben, but it's not there."

"I could . . . I could help you look for it," Jason offered.

He *was* getting a crush on her! She smiled sadly. "No, Jason, you couldn't. Ben wouldn't allow it."

That got through to him. Jason seemed to shrivel up inside of himself. He glanced out the window. "What do you think he's doing?"

"Whatever he wants to do," Lisa replied. "That's what Ben *always* does—exactly what he wants to do." *And it isn't going to get better,* she thought. She was trapped here, in this hot car, in this burning desert, with a greedy coward, an amoral criminal and . . .

And whatever was in that spaceship . . .

CHAPTER 8

THE TENSION IN the command center was getting almost unbearable. Steve fidgeted slightly, trying to relax some of his cramped muscles. His stomach was a knot of anxiety and fear. The Zanti had arrived, but they had not spoken again. What were they doing? What were they planning? Had they seen the intruder? Did they think the humans had betrayed them? Were they even now planning a terrible retaliation?

General Hart slipped on the communications headset again, and spoke. He was trying to keep his voice calm, level and reasonable, but it cracked from time to time due to his own nerves. "This is General Hart to Zanti ship. The person or persons in your landing area are unauthorized. I repeat, they are unauthorized. We would like your permission to enter the restricted area after them to bring them out again and punish them." He waited a moment, but there was no response.

"You are in no danger from the people in your area," Hart

said, his voice less steady now. "They are unauthorized. This is simply an accident. We wish your permission to send in a party to remove them."

Steve couldn't stop wondering how the Zanti were taking this. They must hear Hart's voice. Why were they not replying? Even just to say no? What was going through their alien minds?

The Zanti regent studied the controls of his ship, and then his eyes flickered toward the screens. Inside his command pod, he had 360-degree vision, thanks to the screens both inside and out of the ship. He carefully powered down the drive engines, but didn't cut them entirely. There was always a possibility that there would be a need to take off again.

The irritating human voice was still coming over the speakers. The sound of it made his skin crawl. It was so loud, so aggressive and so grating. "We wish to remove them with no inconvenience to you," the voice said. "Do not suspect us of betraying you. We have kept to our agreement! We have not double-crossed you."

The regent had absolutely no idea what the human was saying, since he'd turned off the translator. It hardly mattered what the humans wanted to say. It was all irrelevant. On the way to the landing, the regent had seen the human vehicle sitting close to the target point. There were humans outside of it, watching the skies. That had been a clear violation of the agreement, and nothing that the humans could say about it could excuse their lack of good faith.

The humans were as bad as the misfits. They were unreliable, possibly treacherous, and unproductive. The regent felt nothing but disgust for them.

His instruments showed him that one of the humans was approaching the penal ship.

For the moment, he would observe. He knew very little

about the humans. It had not been considered necessary to tell
him very much, since he was not supposed to ever meet any
of them in person. So he would watch. And then he would
evaluate the most appropriate response to the intruder.

The regent's mandibles clicked together. His poison sacs
were full.

"There is no need for you to consider retaliating," the human continued. "Believe that. Please . . . believe that!"

Ignoring the attempt at conversation, the regent turned away
to study his screens again. Then, from the Zanti homeworld,
he heard a response to the call. If his face had been able to,
he would have smiled at the reply.

"Fleen zant a mol o van itinsi," it said in calm, measured
tones. Perfectly in meter, perfectly in harmony, the embodi-
ment of Zanti order vocalized. "Lanz trinsini lobo zan a mang
sil lanz ob."

That was exactly what the regent had been hoping for. It
was time for the humans to understand just whom they were
dealing with here.

"They've replied," Hart said, smiling slightly. He glanced
over at the computer technician. "Translate their message."

The technician did so. Steve stared in horror at the speakers
as that grim, grating, inhuman Zanti voice declared: "The
agreement is clear. Total destruction to anyone who invades
our privacy."

No compromise, no appeal: the Zanti were going to strike
back. . . .

Clambering over the last of the rocks, Ben arrived at level
ground again. Below, and almost half a mile away, he could
make out his car, waiting in the desert. Ahead . . .

He stiffened, partly in amazement, partly in shock. There
was the flying saucer, on the ground. It was still humming or

buzzing softly to itself. But it didn't look at all like anything he'd been expecting.

First of all, its shape was odd. He'd been expecting the classic look of the flattened disc that everyone always described and all the movies showed. This wasn't like that at all. It was fat and dumpy, like an overturned children's top, or even a bit like a beehive. It looked to be segmented vertically, and the peak of the ship was of a darker hue than the silvered surface of the rest of it. Around the base of the craft were a series of what had to be windows, though he could see nothing inside of them. Around the base of the ship were short, stubby wings that could hardly be much help in steering the craft through the air. The rockets, or whatever the thing used for propulsion, had to be out of sight underneath the ship.

Added to the strange shape was the size of the thing. He'd been expecting something hundreds if not thousands of feet across. The ship he was staring at was barely as tall as he was. Six feet, tops. And only about four feet at its widest point.

If this *was* a ship from outer space, then it would have to be unmanned—un*aliened*?—or else have very small passengers.

But was it from outer space? The area had been surrounded by human military. Maybe this was a human device. Some kind of spy satellite, maybe? In which case it could be very valuable indeed. Maybe valuable enough for him to be able to make a profit off it. It didn't look as though it would be light enough for him to move, but if he could rig up some kind of explosive on it, he could hold it hostage. Then when the army came after him, he could demand money and safe passage out of the area or he'd destroy their experimental whatsit. Ben grinned. It sounded like a pretty decent plan to him. As always, he could work an angle on any situation he was in. This little device could be his way out of this situation, and with a little added bonus if he were lucky.

Moving forward cautiously, he drew closer to the craft. He could feel a slight surge in heat from the thing. Must have been warmed by its passage through the atmosphere, he realized. No sign of any parachute, so it had to be pretty maneuverable. Should be worth a bundle to the right people . . .

He went down on one knee, and leaned forward to peer into one of the little windows. Then he shook his head. It must be tinted glass, because he couldn't see anything inside there. A vague memory that some satellites used infrared and ultraviolet scanners came back to him. Maybe that's what the windows were for, in fact: to shoot out the scanning rays. He straightened up hastily. The machinery was probably shut down, but there was no sense in taking stupid risks. It was still humming, after all, so *something* inside of it was working.

Ben backed away a few paces, rubbing at his chin and studying the ship. What he needed now was some way to get at its insides. There were vertical ridges running down the craft, but no sign of any access panels or bolts or anything that he could undo to get a look at its insides. Well, he'd go back down to the car and get the tool kit. With that, he might be able to effect an entry into the small ship. . . .

There was another hum, this one louder and deeper in pitch. Something was happening to the ship. Was it sending out some kind of homing signal, so that the army types could come and recover it? No . . . As Ben watched, fascinated, a small section of the ship near the base opened up. It was about six inches square, and simply folded upward inside the ship. A short ramp then slid out to the ground.

Maybe it wasn't a human satellite, then? Was it going to take some sort of soil samples, maybe? Ben bent forward for a better look at whatever was going to emerge from the little hatchway. Fascinating!

And then he gasped, and backed away in horror at what he saw.

It was some kind of living being, that much was clear. And it was something that had never grown up on Earth. And it was *ugly*.

The creature skittered down the ramp, and paused there, surveying Ben as he stared in horror down at it. The creature was vaguely like an ant, at least in general body shape. It had six long, thin legs that held its body a couple of inches off the ramp. Two antennae on its head twitched, focusing on Ben.

But it was the head that was the most disgusting. . . .

It *almost* looked human, rather than antlike. It had a gash for a mouth, with tiny, serrated teeth inside. On either side of the mouth were mandibles, which pulsed slightly as it watched him. And the eyes . . . they were far too large for the head, really, with gleaming pupils that focused on him.

And Ben knew with absolute certainty that whatever this creature was, it was intelligent. It, or its people, had built the small ship, and they had crossed space to come here. It was looking at him, and he knew that it had a ferociously keen brain.

And in those eyes, Ben could read implacable hatred, so strong it almost burned him.

For the first time in his life, Ben knew real fear. A fear of the unknown, a fear of the stranger, and a fear of death. The creature facing him was intelligent and it found him as disgusting as he found it. Ben whimpered in the back of his throat and started to edge away from the craft. All thoughts of making a deal, of creating an advantage, were gone. All he wanted to do now was to escape.

The creature lunged forward, scuttling like an ant or a spider across the hot rocks.

Ben panicked and tried to run. But the rocks under his feet

were loose, and he had to glance down to keep his balance. He lost sight of the creature, and was forced to grab at a large boulder to regain his balance. Then he glanced around. The craft was still there, but he couldn't see the little monster anywhere. Where had it gone?

Something touched his hand, and he whirled around, re-coiling in terror. The thing had dropped from the rock onto his hand.

"Get off me!" he screamed, feeling the tiny feet gripping his skin tightly. "Get off me!" He couldn't think clearly. All that mattered was for the thing to be gone! He screamed once, and struck at the creature with his free hand.

The thing hissed at him, the mandibles snapping together, barely missing his fingers, the antennae twitching. Then it scuttled up his arm, toward his shoulder.

"No! Don't!" Ben screamed, flailing, trying to dislodge the thing, but without luck. The small feet held on without effort as it moved up his arm. "Help!" Ben howled. "Somebody help me!"

The creature hissed again, and leaped for his face.

Inside the command center, everyone had fallen silent. The speakers had come to life again, carrying a message from the Zanti ship. But it wasn't from the Zanti. The human intruder must have found the ship, Steve realized. And the Zanti had promised immediate and total destruction. . . .

"No!" a man's voice yelled, its tones soaked in fear and revulsion. "Get off me! Help! Help me, somebody!"

And then the man screamed, a long, drawn-out cry of pure terror that choked off suddenly.

Leaving only silence across the static hiss.

CHAPTER 9

LISA DIDN'T KNOW what to do. Her mind was such a tumbled mess of conflicting emotions and thoughts. The face of the dead guard, the burning expression in Ben's eyes, the heat radiating all around her that soaked her clothes with sweat. Jason, panting behind her. From heat? Fear? Or something else? She traced the crack in the windshield with a finger, aimlessly, staring out at the desert.

She only hoped that the army would come for them soon. Or even the police. Either way, she'd get out of this heat into a nice cool cell somewhere. Out of these clothes that should have been changed days ago. Maybe even into a shower or a bath. She smiled gently. She could stand being arrested, if it involved being able to clean herself again, finally.

The thought of water made her realize that she was thirsty. Ben had replaced the flask in the glove compartment. She opened it up, and a couple of bundles of bills fell into her lap, then onto the floor. Ignoring them, she pulled out the flask and unscrewed the top. She took a long drink—

Except that there was just a single mouthful left. As usual, Ben had taken what he'd wanted, leaving nothing for anyone else. With a sigh, she swallowed what little there had been. Jason was out of luck if he was thirsty. Recapping the flask, she replaced it in the glove compartment.

She hoped it wouldn't be long until they were found.

In a sudden burst of energy, she snapped on the radio. Maybe there would be a news show on that might tell her something. She adjusted the station to the local news channel.

A commercial jingle was just ending, and then the news reader came on. He sounded cheery and cool. *He* probably had a big carafe of water right next to his microphone, the lucky so-and-so.

"And, as usual in the hot weather, it looks like all the flying saucer nuts have been at it again," the man said. She could hear the grin in his voice. "Half of southern California seems to have called in UFO sightings today. This station's clocked about thirty calls so far. We tried to get an official response, but, as usual, all we were told is that nothing has been detected. NASA officials say *they* haven't tracked anything. Neither the police nor the local army and air force bases have, either, it seems.

"In other words, folks, whatever you *think* you saw, it *isn't* what you think you saw. If you can believe the official word, of course. Unless, of course, any of you good folks out there that didn't see it also got a photo or videotape of whatever it was that wasn't there. If you did, just call five-five-five-three-one-three-one and we'll be glad to—"

She clicked the radio off again, suddenly worried. She'd been trying to avoid thinking about the thing they'd seen. That silver flash of whatever-it-was coming down from the sky and into the nearby ridge. The one that Ben had gone off to investigate . . .

Lisa opened the door and climbed out. The hot air clung to her skin, and she started to sweat again. "Ben?" she called, looking toward the rocks. There was no reply. "Ben?" she called, louder this time.

"You think he's okay?" asked Jason nervously.

"He's Ben," Lisa replied. "He's *always* okay. Still . . ." She glanced back at Jason. "Stay in the car," she said gently. He'd be no use to her if he came with her. He was already scared of his own shadow. If there *was* something out there . . . She swallowed, trying to keep down the panic that was growing inside of her. Ben was out there. Maybe she didn't like him very much, but she couldn't simply abandon him. Especially not if he were in trouble. "I'll be back as soon as I can," she promised. She started to move off.

"You be careful," Jason advised her. He hadn't protested at being left behind at all.

"I surely will," Lisa told him. Then she set off for the ridge where Ben had vanished. She could hear a faint humming in the air. It had to be coming from whatever that thing was that nobody official supposedly knew anything about. If they didn't, then how come they were here with armed guards? That had to be some kind of secret project, and they'd just stumbled across it by accident.

She could only hope that they'd be allowed to stumble out again.

Steve watched Hart as he spoke to the president on the red hot line. "No, sir," the general said firmly. "I cannot advise you to order any further intervention in that area. Whoever did manage to get in there has already shot our credibility with the Zanti sky-high. If we were to go in after him, they would most likely construe it as an offensive, and perhaps retaliatory, measure on our part. At best, it would deepen their suspicions and further weaken our relationship. At worst . . .'' His voice trailed off. He nodded at something the president said.

"I realize that, sir,'' he said. "But we don't even know if the man's still alive. That scream sounded pretty terminal to me. They may have destroyed him instantly. In which case, if we went in, we'd be accomplishing nothing, and touching off heaven knows what!''

There was another outburst from the president, and Hart flinched. "No, sir, I am not allowing myself to be prejudiced. I can't overlook the fact that he killed one of my men, either by accident or design. But because I don't know whether the act was intentional or not, I can't say whether the man's a killer or simply someone who panicked and ran when he saw what he had done. I'm not making a judgment as to his possible rescue based on those factors, sir.''

Hart was definitely getting a battering, Steve realized. The president was clearly advocating sending troops into the area. He was probably worried about the fallout if the public discovered that he had allowed the Zanti to kill a human being without making *some* effort to save the man's life. But in this case, Steve was on the general's side. That scream . . . Steve shuddered. It had been the desperate howl of a dying man, he was sure of that. And it had stopped because the man was dead.

"Sir,'' Hart said firmly, "I simply do not want to start anything with the Zanti!'' He listened a moment, and then added, "We have the channel still open. If they decide to reestablish contact, then we're ready.'' Another pause as he listened. Wearily, he said, "Yes, sir. Fifteen minutes. If they do not communicate within the next quarter of an hour . . .'' He handed the phone back to the soldier he'd assigned to monitor the line. ". . . then God help us,'' he finished softly.

He looked at Steve and then at Hill, and his eyes were even more tired.

"Fifteen minutes is not a long time," Hill said gently. "In our conception of time. For them . . . it could be long enough for them to conquer a world."

The general stared at Hill for a moment, and then turned away, his shoulders slumping. He walked slowly into the other room, pushing through the beaded curtain.

Steve felt a twinge of sympathy for his father's old friend. This assignment had been rough enough to begin with, but it was getting worse and worse. Hart was literally on the firing line here. Anything he did might cause an interplanetary war. And if he did nothing, then the president was ready to overrule him and order troops in. Well, the president had to worry about his image and his career. He seemed to be oblivious to the fact that Hart was thinking in terms of the survival of the human race, not simply how the newspapers and TV reporters would publicize events.

Hill shook his head. "When a country allows itself to be coerced, as we have done, it has to suffer the consequences." He was obviously feeling that he'd been right about the Zanti from the very beginning.

"So far," Steve pointed out, "the only real consequence is uncertainty."

Hill stared at him, his eyes cold and dark. "I have always felt," he said softly, "that uncertainty is one of the worst things a country could suffer."

There was no answer to that, so Steve didn't even try. Hill's paranoid feelings were clearly growing. And with good reason, Steve knew. The Zanti had done precisely what they had promised—they had destroyed the intruder into their territory. But would they be satisfied with that? Or would they retaliate against the rest of the human race? General Hart had to be going through the private torments of Hell right now. He might need someone to talk to.

Steve went into the other room to join the general. The older man was at the soda machine again, and was once more struggling to free a can from the machine's embrace. Steve smiled slightly, his first smile in quite a while. Same old Max . . . Steve gently pushed him aside, and withdrew the cola can. Popping it, he handed it to the general. Then he got one for himself.

"Maybe they've taken the man into their ship," he suggested, striving for anything to reassure Hart. He didn't really believe it himself, but it *was* possible. "If they believe his ignorance, they'll probably reopen communication with us."

Hart took a swig of soda, and then brushed at his short hair. "I don't mind a dilemma, Steve," he said, as if from nowhere. "Not when I have some knowledge of my enemy."

Uncertainty, Steve thought. He managed a crooked grin, and then said, "Quoting General Max Hart: 'So far as we know, the inhabitants of the planet Zanti are not our enemy.' Unquote."

Hart shook his head. "They *are*," he said firmly. "Anyone who blackmails and coerces and forces their will upon us is an enemy. What I said before, I said because I *had* to, Steve. It's the official line. Now . . . well, now the official line might not mean very much anymore. And I *don't* like them. I don't respect them. I pretended to do so, but no longer. I was just trying to minimize the problem by saying that I did." He took another drink of cola.

"I hate all enemies of our country, Steve. That's my job, and I believe in it. And the Zanti aren't only *our* enemies, they're the enemies of all human beings on this planet. Right now, I would like to go in there, pick up the hot line and advise the president to destroy that ship." He looked Steve straight in the eyes, and Steve knew he was being told the truth. Then the general's shoulders slumped slightly again. "I would like to do that. But I can't."

"Why not?" asked Steve quietly. "If you did, I don't think there's a man or woman here who would say you were wrong."

"Because I'm afraid." Hart straightened up again. "And I'm old. And I'm sick to death of all of this. If we destroy their ship, they are bound to retaliate. And that will mean war. It will mean death and suffering." He gestured toward the other room. "You've seen them, Steve. Those *kids* out there are younger even than you. They have their lives ahead of them. So does the rest of the human race. If I commit to destroying the Zanti ship, then *they* are the ones who'll pay for it. It will mean broken bodies and broken hearts if I give that order." He shook his head. "I can't do it. I can't let everybody break like that. I can't give an order that might start the most horrendous war this world has ever known. One that might even mean the end of the human race. I *have* to keep this thing bottled up here."

"Then I've got a suggestion," Steve said.

"If you have," Hart answered, "believe me, I'd love to hear it. Anything to end this uncertainty."

"An emissary," Steve said. Hart blinked, and started to look interested. "Tell them that you're sending in *one* man, alone and unarmed, who is fully informed and prepared to discuss the situation with them personally. Tell them that this emissary will arrive in an open vehicle so that they can ensure the terms are being met. Tell them he'll halt and then advance when and only if instructed to do so." He touched the general's arm. "They may decide to keep silent, even after hearing that. But at least they'll know what your intentions are. And that we want to find a peaceful solution to this problem."

Hart considered the idea. "But will we know what their intentions are?" he asked. "If they keep silent, will we know whether or not they'll let my emissary approach?''

"No," Steve said. "You'll have to take a risk there. But you have to take a risk whatever you decide to do.''

"*I'll* have to take a risk?" Hart said cynically. "What about the man I'll have to send? There's no way I can leave here and do the job myself. I have to be here to make the decisions should . . . anything happen.''

"*You* have to take a risk," Steve repeated. "And *I* will. You make the decision. I'll go.''

"You?" Hart stared at him in surprise. "Why you?''

"I've studied history for years, Max," Steve said. He didn't want to beg for this chance, but he knew he might get awfully close. "Even before I was supposed to at school. Hearing you and Dad talking about great events, all that you'd seen and experienced . . . big moments, small moments, some so insignificant that they just barely got recorded. I've heard so many stories, studied so many stories, written up so many. But it isn't like being there! I'm always a spectator and never a participant. I'm always conscious of that, always aware of what I'm missing. I'd give anything just to *be* there, just once, alive and awake! I don't want to be here and now, standing on the edge of history, only to pull back without touching the event. I don't want them, when they write this one up for the history books, to say 'Oh, and Steve Grave was there, watching.' I want to be a part of this, Max, so badly you probably can't understand it.''

Max smiled faintly. "I suppose you'd like to have been there for Desert Storm, too.''

"If I could have helped," Steve answered fervently. "Look, Max, you've been there, done things I can only read about. What have I done with my life, except to record the actions of other people?''

Max shook his head. "No, Steve.''

Anger, frustration and fear burned inside of Steve. He

stopped paying careful attention to what he was saying, and simply went with the first things in his head. "My father wouldn't have let me go out to that spaceship, either," he said bitterly. "He never let me go anywhere that wasn't guaranteed safe. Maybe that's why I turned to reading history books—at least there something happened."

The general gazed at him with sympathy. "It's not your job, Steve."

"Yes, it is!" Steve cried. "It's *exactly* my job. I'm a professor of communications, and communication with the Zanti is what we most need right now. Max, if *this* isn't my job, then nothing ever will be!"

"You don't know what you'd be getting into," Hart objected, clearly losing ground under the force of Steve's emotional outburst.

"No," Steve agreed, surprising the general. "I *don't* know. That's the whole point. That's why I want to go. For once in my life, I want to experience something that hasn't already happened. I don't want to *read* about it, or stand by while someone else does the job. I want it to be *me* that does what's needed. And I honestly believe that there's no one more qualified for this job on this base than me, Max. I know it sounds like I'm asking from a selfish need here, but I would never endanger this mission—the whole human race—just to fulfill some selfish need. I'm the best man for this job, period."

The general thought about this and then sighed. "I'd better tell the patrols to allow you through, then," he decided.

Steve cracked a wide grin, nodded eagerly, and then followed the general back into the mission room. Finally, he was getting the chance he had always wanted. He was going to be a part of this, after all. He was going to get his chance to meet the Zanti, face to face.

The only downside to the whole thing was that the only human being so far to have met the Zanti appeared to have been killed. What were Steve's chances of surviving such an encounter?

Lisa was beyond second thoughts now. Every ten feet, she considered going back. The whine of the whatever-it-was was growing louder as she climbed through the rocks toward where Ben had vanished from her sight earlier. Then she would stop, and call out his name. It would echo about the rocks without reply. And she would stand there, looking in vain for any movement, wondering if something had happened to Ben or he was simply not bothering to reply. That would be quite like him. Her feelings were irrelevant to him, and if he didn't want to answer her frantic calls, then he wouldn't.

As she always did, though, after a short pause, she moved onward. Lisa wasn't even sure why she was bothering to look for Ben at all. All her emotions for him had been burned away, just like the grass and plant life had been burned from this desert. All that was left of her now was the underlying rock and sand of her personality. Nothing living, nothing vital; just the dregs.

What did she want out of life? She'd never really known. Just not what she had. Rich parents might seem like a blessing to some kids, but never to her. They were both control freaks who insisted on overseeing every last little item in her life. She'd been allowed no growth of her own. Everything had been calculated, ordered and seen to. Lisa had been allowed no choice in the matter. That was why Ben had so attracted her. There was nothing at all about him that was ordered, disciplined or controlled. His emotions were never hidden away, and his needs were blatant and worn upon his sleeve. He had excited her, and she had run away from home with him without a look back.

But now, she had discovered, Ben was as shallow as her parents had been. His was simply a different kind of shallowness, a harder, more dangerous kind. Her first hints of that had been the punches when she'd done something he didn't like. And there was a lot he didn't like. At first, even the blows had been welcome to Lisa. At least it meant that she was accomplishing something, that she mattered enough for him to hit her. But then she had realized that his "reasons" for what he did were simply lies. He hit her not because she deserved it, but simply because he enjoyed it.

And that violent streak in him had grown worse. The teller he had killed—Lisa now knew that that had been a deliberate action. It hadn't been from a moment of panic. Ben had probably simply wanted to see somebody die. And she had seen in his eyes and face his decision to kill that guard, even before the man had tried to stop them. Whatever Ben had said after either killing was just excuses. The fact was, he *wanted* to kill.

And Lisa knew, with absolute clarity and certainty, that if she stayed with him, he would kill her, too, sooner or later. The best thing she could do would be to leave him and give herself up to the army, the police or anyone at all. Admit what she had done, and accept the punishment she deserved. That was the smartest thing she could do.

So—why, then, was she scrambling across hot rocks in the desert, ruining her already ratty sneakers and filthy jeans, breaking her nails and looking for Ben? Had something happened to him? Good! Then she'd be free of him, past the point where he could hurt her any more. This was really dumb. She shouldn't be here, hunting him out. For all she knew, he might be *deliberately* hiding from her, waiting just over those next rocks with that gun in his hand, having decided that she was now more trouble than she was worth to keep around. She might just be walking into a trap; he might be waiting there, that nasty little grin on his face, gun level and just waiting for her grime-spatted face to appear in view . . .

She clambered over the rocks anyway. There was no reason for what she was doing that she could think of. She simply *had* to know. If Ben was dead, somehow, and she was free, she wanted to see it with her own eyes, to be sure of it. If it were a trick, and he was going to kill her—well, at least she would know that, too. She wasn't afraid of dying, not when there was so much more pain in simply going on living. And if Ben was simply absorbed in whatever he was doing and just ignoring her, then she wanted to know that, too. She was sick of being in the dark with him. She wanted just one honest, decent emotion. Death, murder, or simply indifference. She wanted to know where she stood in his life.

And then she saw him. He was on the ground, in the shade of some rocks, curled up in a fetal position, unmoving.

Shock ran through her. "Ben," she called, but there was no response, not even any movement. Had he fallen and knocked himself out? Had he been attacked? Or was this some trick of his for some twisted reason? She staggered upward, and made her way to where he lay.

He was dead. That much was quite clear, even before she drew close to the body. His skin was blotched around his neck, a deep, disgusting purple color, edged with bile yellow. His veins looked as if they'd been etched on his face and neck in black ink. His mouth was open in a silent scream, and his eyes bulged.

Something had killed him . . .

Lisa's heart was pounding ferociously, and not from the effort of the climb. Shaking, she reached out to try to turn his body over, to avoid seeing those terrible eyes. What could have done this to him? A snake? A scorpion, maybe? They had them out here in the desert, she knew. But she'd seen no sign of life at all. She felt no anger or pity for Ben. All her emotions for him were long gone. He was simply Ben, now dead. But what if whatever had killed him was still around?

She drew her hand back nervously from the corpse without touching him. It might not be safe . . .

With a hiss, something launched itself from the shadows where it had been hiding, towards her hand. It was spiderlike, with a dreadful, human kind of face, and it was trying to *bite* her. Lisa pulled back with a scream, and fell backward.

The Zanti pounced.

CHAPTER 10

THE REGENT HAD waited beside the body of the first human intruder, knowing that if there were more of them, they would come and investigate the one he had killed. As he had suspected, another one had arrived.

They were disgusting, these humans. No wonder the Zanti government had never released any pictures of them. They were dreadful monstrosities, misshapen and overly large. Gigantic beasts, that's what they were. They had too few legs to be stable or nimble. Their eyes were too small in proportion to their faces, and they lacked mandibles and poison sacs. Their features were crude and their bodies disgusting in their pallid whiteness.

After killing the first human, the regent had slithered inside its clothing, taking his measure of the man. A weak and puny body, with no natural defenses. Why, even in this heat, the creature had to wear cloth over its body! Either for warmth or for modesty. Well, if he had a body that disgusting, he'd want to keep it covered up, too.

As the second human approached, he watched it from the shadows where he waited. It was very similar to the first one, though it had additional deformities. Its chest, for one thing, was swollen, as if it were sick. And that long stuff on the top of its head was lighter in color and longer than on the dead human. It looked even more monstrous and alien than the first. But it looked just as puny and defenseless.

The newcomer moved toward the body, and extended its hand. Just a little closer . . . The regent coiled his muscles, ready to spring.

And then the alien monster started to draw back. Had it seen him somehow? The regent didn't think so, but there was still a chance. Hissing its battle cry, it leaped from concealment at the outstretched limb. The human's mouth opened, and its high-pitched cry came out. But it was quicker than the regent had expected, and his leap failed to contact it. He landed nimbly on the rocks, and coiled for a further leap.

The human whirled and fled, half falling and half running. The regent considered leaping after it, but it was in the direct sun, and that could be dangerous. Unshielded as he was, the regent would quickly overheat in the burning sun of this arid region. Instead of following the alien and running the risk of overheating, he whirled and scuttled back to the ship.

Once inside, he lifted off, tilting the craft to stay close to the ground. The human was retreating, and there was only one place logically that it must be heading: back to the road vehicle he had seen when he was landing. All he had to do was to get to the vehicle, and then he would have the other human intruder. As he had sworn, and as Zanti control had commanded, all intruders would be dealt with.

It was only a matter of time. The regent was enjoying himself. He had always enjoyed hunting his prey. . . .

*　　*　　*

Hart spoke slowly and clearly into the microphone in the control center. "Our emissary will be unarmed and will await your permission to advance. He will wait for one hour. If he does not receive your permission within that time, he will return to the base without any further attempt to reach you. Permit this man to approach you. It is vital to your own security that we know your precise mood and intentions, just as it is vital to you to know ours. I send this man with reluctance and trepidation—but also with hope." He clicked off the microphone, removed the headset and handed it back to the technician. Then he turned to Steve.

"Well, that's it," he said with a deep sigh. "We know that the Zanti heard our message. All we can do now is let you go, and hope that they will make the best decision. It's what a logical man would do. But who knows how the Zanti will behave?"

"We'll find out in the next hour, General," Steve answered.

Major Hill returned to the room, a slight smile on his face. "The jeep's waiting out front for you, Professor," he said. "There's a radio in it so you can keep in touch with us—and with the Zanti, if they choose to communicate. We'll have to do all of the translating here, of course, and transmit it to you. There's also a megaphone, for when you reach the area. Plus water—you're going to need that out there while you're waiting. And a little food. Military rations, so you won't get fat on them. Just in case. I doubt you'll be out there past the hour, but it's better to be prepared."

"Thank you, Major," Steve replied. Hill was clearly very efficient and careful. "I appreciate it."

Hill nodded. "I'd bet you'll just sit there for the hour and then come back," he said. "This may not be the adventure you're after."

"Maybe not," agreed Steve. "But I'll only find out one way."

"Good luck."

"Right, Steve," agreed the general. "Take no chances. If things seem wrong in any way out there, don't be embarrassed to turn tail and run. We'll be monitoring you constantly, and if we have to, we'll provide covering fire." He grimaced. "I only hope we don't have to."

"Me, too," Steve agreed. "I'd hate to have to dodge friendly fire." With a nod, he headed for the door. The guard respectfully opened it. Steve stepped outside. As Hill had promised, the Jeep awaited him, its motor humming softly.

It was now or never. Steve had been perfectly serious in what he had told the general. But despite his best intentions, he couldn't help feeling fear and apprehension as well. He'd talked himself into this job. Now he had to pray that he'd survive it.

Lisa scrambled and clawed her way back down the rocks and toward the desert floor below. She kept looking back over her shoulder, but there was no sign at all of the dreadful, ugly alien thing she had seen on Ben's corpse. It had been so hideous, with that insectlike body and the humanoid face. It had also been deliberately hiding, hoping to kill her. She'd survived the attack only by accident, and she was absolutely certain that it had no intention of simply giving up just because she had escaped the first attack.

She broke free of the rocks at last. In front of her was the car, and safety. She could lock the doors and keep the creature out. The army would be along soon. They were bound to find the body of that guard and come after the intruders. All she had to do was hold out until they arrived. Then she'd be safe.

Gasping for breath, her legs hurting where she'd lacerated them on the rocks when she'd fallen, Lisa grimly concentrated only on getting back to the car. She focused on that, running as fast as she could. Every step was painful, but it was better than dying. Her lungs burned, her chest ached, her legs were on fire. But safety was just ahead of her.

Then she heard the whine of the spaceship increase in volume. She risked looking back over her shoulder and almost fainted with shock. The ship she'd glimpsed before was hovering over the rocky formation behind her! She'd thought that all she had to do was escape the creature, forgetting entirely about the ship. Did it have some death ray in it that would wipe out her and the car from a distance? Vague, jumbled thoughts of the movies she'd seen of alien invaders flitted through her mind. Laser beams, tractor beams, death rays . . . *anything* like that could be in that ship. She staggered to a halt, wondering if it were even worth bothering trying to escape. The creature could do anything with a ship like that.

And then the craft settled down again, this time well in view, perched in the shadows on the close side of the rocky formation.

Lisa, gasping for breath, stared at it. It wasn't going to use its weapons on the car, then. So why had it made the short flight? And why was it just sitting there? Shielding her eyes, she stared at the hive-shaped ship.

A small door opened in the side of it, and she saw a scuttling form run out. And then she knew.

The creature had used the ship to get closer to her, for some reason. It was now going to try to catch her . . .

Whirling, she ran as fast as she could for the car. She didn't dare look back. That alien creature was *fast*. Lisa ran because her life depended upon it. If it beat her back to the car, she was doomed.

Jason must have been watching for her. He opened the rear door and stepped out. "Lisa?" he called. "What's happening? What *is* that flying saucer? What's it doing?"

"Get back in the car!" she screamed, with what little breath she could spare. "Now!" He didn't understand her, but he must have heard the panic and urgency in her voice because he hopped inside and closed the door again.

Lisa reached the car just before her legs gave out on her. She dragged herself inside, and then slammed the door shut. She hit the door lock, and curled up in her seat, fighting for breath.

"What is it, Lisa?" Jason asked, picking up her panic. "What's going on?"

"Ben's dead," she said, panting and scanning the desert outside the car for a sign of anything. "Some . . . *thing* killed him. It's got a poisonous bite. He was . . ." She shook her head. Her chest was heaving, but she was getting her breath back. Her pulse was racing, though, and she could hear the rush of blood in her ears. "It's after *us* now. But if we stay in the car, we'll be safe. It won't be able to reach us."

Jason turned his frightened eyes on the landscape also. "What's this thing look like?" he asked.

"You'll see it for yourself in a moment," she promised him. "It came after me."

And then there was a slight shudder as the creature leaped onto the car. It stood there, on the hood, staring in at them through the windshield. Lisa heard Jason give a gasp. It sounded like he wanted to throw up. But she couldn't take her eyes off the alien as it slowly walked up the hood of the car and toward the windshield. Its eyes were fixed on her, and it appeared to have some purpose in mind.

What would it try next?

Steve cut the engine of the jeep as he braked to a halt. He surveyed the rocks ahead of him, but there was no sign of movement. He wished he'd thought to bring some kind of hat to shield his eyes from the glare of the sun. After a fruitless moment, he turned to the radio, and picked up the micro-phone.

"This is Grave," he said into it. "I've reached the area where the Zanti ship landed, but I can't see anything. It's really broken up here, so the craft could be anywhere."

"Okay, Steve," Hart's voice came back. "We've had some odd readings on the ground radar. It looks like the ship may have shifted position slightly. We figure it's on the far side of that mound of rocks from you right now. But I wouldn't advise trying to get any closer."

"I agree, General," Steve answered. "I'll try to contact them now. Let me know if this works."

He picked up the megaphone, and switched it on. "This is the human emissary," he said into it, and he heard its metallic tones echo about the rocks. "I am in position as I promised. I cannot see your ship. I will not try to. I will await your signal to advance." He paused, but there was no indication of anything at all. "I am in radio contact with General Hart," he continued. "If you tell him I may advance, he will inform me. Otherwise, I will wait one hour and then go away." He clicked off the speaker, and replaced it on the back seat of the jeep.

Shielding his eyes, he scanned the rocks again. Still nothing. Wondering if he had come out here to do nothing more than sit out in the sun, he sat down and tried to compose himself to wait patiently.

It was going to be a very long hour.

Lisa couldn't take her eyes off the horrible creature as it clambered onto the windshield. Like an insect, it seemed to have no problems at all walking on the glass. Her skin crawled as she saw it, barely a foot from her face. It was close enough for her to see the fine hairs that covered its body now, and to see the inhuman glint in its eyes.

It was a look she'd seen before, in Ben's eyes sometimes, right before Ben had hurt someone.

This creature was enjoying hunting them. It was filled with a desire to kill. Perhaps to it, humans were ugly, disgusting creatures. But Lisa didn't care. All she knew was that it was gross, and that it wanted her dead.

"Oh, God," said Jason weakly, from the rear seat. "It's trying to kill us."

"It can't get in," Lisa said, trying to sound firm. "As long as it's out there and we're in here, we're safe."

The thing seemed to know that as well. She could hear it hissing to itself as it moved across the glass. Then it reached the point where the guard's body had cracked the glass, and it halted. Standing over the crack, it bent its head down, opening its mandibles.

It lunged forward, slamming the mandibles against the glass.

The crack widened slightly.

Lisa panicked. They *weren't* safe in the car! The thing had found the weak spot! It was going to break the glass so that it could get in after them. Then they wouldn't be safe inside the car—they'd be trapped.

Inside the Zanti penal ship, there was movement. The regent had departed the craft again, leaving only the two subregents behind with the misfits. The subregents had small quarters behind the command deck. From here, they could survey the cells holding the prisoners. The doors to the cells were under their command, and were never supposed to be opened for any reason.

The two Zanti looked at one another, and then spoke briefly. When they had finished, their front legs started to tap control sequences into the panel.

* * *

Hart waited impatiently inside the command center. He hated being out of the action, but he was needed here right now. What were the Zanti up to? Why had they moved their ship such a short distance? Would they reply to Steve's message?

Moving to join him, Hill said quietly, "That move took their ship out of range of the buried explosives, General. Do you think they detected them, and moved accordingly?"

"I hope not," Hart grunted. "If they *did* detect them, it won't make them any happier with us."

"That's not what bothers me the most," the major answered. "What worries me is that we have no way to destroy that ship of theirs where it lies now without calling in a missile strike." He didn't have to add that while Steve was in the area, that would not be an easy call to make.

"There shouldn't be any need to destroy the Zanti, Major," Hart said. But his statement lacked a lot of his previous conviction.

"There shouldn't be any need for a lot of things," Hill agreed. "But the Zanti have killed a human being. They may be beyond being reasonable—if they ever had intentions of doing so in the first place."

And then they heard the Zanti again. The voice sounded slightly different, so it might have been a different one speaking. But Hart couldn't be certain of that. It could just have been atmospherics, or any number of other reasons.

"Blee olf a ob stra ob purisi dol fang laz, timini strodol ob stra," the voice grated. Hart winced as it spoke. Was this the answer that they had been praying for? Was this permission for Steve to move in and make friendly contact?

He glowered at the technicians. "Translate that!" he snapped. "Quickly!"

A moment later, the speakers came to life again with the translated Zanti voice. "The regent has gone after the other human being. Our opportunity is now. Let us take freedom.''

Hart went pale, as he stared at Hill. "*Other* human being . . ." he repeated in a weak voice.

"There must have been two people in that car," Hill said. "One of them is still alive. But the Zanti's gone after him or her . . ."

Hart's mind was a jumble of thoughts. Too much was happening too quickly. He had to take action, and immediately. He grabbed up the headset again, and ordered the technician: "Contact Professor Grave!" Steve had to be warned. . . .

CHAPTER 11

STEVE TOOK A long sip of the cold water, re-capped the canteen and placed it back in the shade behind his seat. Still nothing at all . . . He checked his watch. He'd been here for fifteen minutes, without any indication that anything was happening. He wished again he'd brought a hat. And maybe even a magazine to read.

Then the radio sprang to life. "Hart to Grave, come in."

Snatching up the microphone, he switched it on. Was this word at last? "Grave here," he replied, eager and apprehensive at once.

"Have you seen the intruder car?" the general asked.

So, no word from the Zanti . . . Steve buried his disappointment and glanced around. "No. It must be on the other side of the outcropping."

"We think there's another person out there, who may still be alive," Hart informed him.

Another person? Steve felt a knot of fear in his stomach.

"Do you want me to have a look around?" he offered. He had promised the Zanti he'd wait where he was, but if there was another intruder out there, that could change the whole game.

"No," the general replied.

"No?" Steve couldn't believe what he'd heard. "You want me to just leave whoever it is out here to maybe be killed by the Zanti?"

"You'd better come back, Steve," Hart said, weariness and resignation in his voice.

This was making less and less sense to Steve every moment. "Come back? But *why*? I've only been here fifteen minutes."

There was a pause, and then Hart explained. "We overheard another transmission from the Zanti ship. Not an official one. The prisoners are going to try to make a break." He paused and then his tired voice finished, "We're going to have to destroy the ship. As soon as you're clear of the area, I'm sending in a missile. So—get out, now!"

Steve didn't know what to do. The whole plan was crashing down around them. The Zanti prisoners were planning a mass break, there was another intruder still at large and there was no talking to the Zanti. He knew he should obey the general, but the thought of leaving another human being out here to die was too much for him. He simply couldn't bring himself to do it.

"Did you hear me, Steve?" Hart demanded.

"Yes," Steve answered calmly. "I heard you." He didn't say he would obey, though.

"Get out of there!" Hart insisted.

Steve stared out at the rocky outcropping. As he did so, he heard the unmistakable sound of a female scream. His eyes widened. "A woman," he murmured. And in desperate trouble.

Making up his mind, he replaced the microphone, and started the jeep's engine. In seconds, he was roaring around the rocks, heading toward where he had heard the scream.

The creature on the windshield rapped the glass again, and the original crack now became a river of larger splits. At any second, the glass would shatter completely, and the thing would have access to them.

Lisa tried to think clearly. The car was now a trap, no longer safe. She had to take her chances outside. Maybe it couldn't run far or fast. Maybe she could outrun it. *Anything*, rather than sit here and wait for it to get her! She unlocked the door, and turned to Jason in the back.

"We've got to run for it," she told him, her voice thin and shrill with fear. "Otherwise we're dead." Jason just moaned, his eyes fixed on the spiderwebbed glass. "Come on!" she snarled. She threw open the door and dived outside, rolling away from the car and scrambling quickly to her feet. She glanced back and saw that the thing was still on the windshield—and that Jason had climbed into the front seat of the car. "Come on!" she screamed to him. "What are you doing?"

"The money," he gasped, grabbing it from where it had spilled onto the carpet. "I'm coming."

But it was too late. The creature gave a final blow on the glass, and the whole windshield exploded into fragments. Lisa saw a blur of movement, and the small black creature landed on Jason's neck.

Her own scream drowned out Jason's gasped cry as the alien bit him as it had bitten Ben.

There was nothing she could do for Jason now. Lisa whirled and ran away from the car, hysterical and drenched with sweat and fear. Both Ben and Jason were dead, and she *knew* that creature was coming after her next. It enjoyed killing people, and it would not allow her to escape.

In fact, there *was* no escape for her. Her legs were weak from her previous strain, and she'd opened several of her cuts again with her dive from the car. She was dehydrated from the sun, and gasping for breath already. She staggered as she ran, and looked back at the car.

Jason's body was hanging from the doorway, twenty-dollar bills trickling from his lifeless fingers. There was no sign of the creature that had killed him. It had to be on her trail now. But she couldn't see it. It was too small, and there was too much cover on the ground, in the form of rocks and crevices. It could be anywhere right now.

She had almost reached the rocks, but she couldn't keep running. There were red blotches before her eyes, and her lungs were on fire. Her legs wobbled, and she couldn't prevent herself from falling. She stumbled and hit the ground. She simply didn't have the strength to stand up again. She crawled for cover amongst the boulders and rocks. Gasping, she brushed the matted hair from her eyes, and stared around. Where was that killer alien? It had to be coming for her.

Then she heard a new sound, that of a car engine. Finally, someone in authority! She knew she should feel happy about being rescued, but she simply didn't have any emotions left to her. They had all been drained out of her through the heat and the fear.

The newcomer stopped, just out of sight, and she heard a man's voice call out: "I'm here to help you! To take you back! You can't stay here! Where are you?"

Lisa wanted to answer, but she could hardly catch her breath, let alone scream a reply. Her chest was still heaving, her heart racing. She was too weak to even make it to her feet.

"We're going to destroy this area!" the man called. "You

have to get out! Let me take you out! No one will hurt you!''

That was almost funny to Lisa. ''No one ever has,'' she whispered to herself. ''Except . . . myself.'' She'd always done the worst possible thing, it seemed. Her whole life had been one dreadful mistake after another, and now here she was—huddled against a rock in some nameless desert, being stalked by a murderous alien that had already killed both of her companions.

Was this justice? After all, she'd been a part of Ben's actions, even if she hadn't known about them or approved them. She'd known what Ben was capable of, and she'd gone along with him regardless. She was hardly innocent. There was blood on her hands, as much as on his. Maybe it was time that she faced up to her own guilt.

There was a blur of movement, and then the creature was there, on a rock some ten feet away, staring at her with those grotesque, huge eyes. The mandibles clicked together, and she knew it was getting ready to spring.

''No, Ben,'' Lisa whispered, unable to take her eyes off the thing. ''I'm not afraid to die.'' *Come and get me, then,* she willed the creature. If she had to die, then so be it. She was through with running. She'd face the consequences of her actions at last.

In the face of death, she felt an odd kind of peace.

Steve saw a vague movement out of the corner of his eye as he approached the rocks. He could see the car from where he'd parked the jeep, and the body hanging out of it. But that was a male corpse; he had definitely heard a female scream. Was she still alive? Or had the Zanti already dealt with her? Why didn't she answer his calls? Was she too frightened? Would her voice give away her position? Did she fear him as much as the alien? After all, if she went back with him, there was still the death of the guard to account for.

Or was she already dead, and was he risking his life for nothing?

The blur of movement resolved itself into a smallish, black *thing* that perched on a rock, staring at something he couldn't see. Steve suddenly knew that this had to be one of the Zanti. It was smaller, much smaller, than he had expected. And it was *ugly*. He shivered, despite the heat; it looked far worse than he had imagined.

And it was clearly hunting someone, which had to be the woman he'd heard. He ran forward quietly, and then he could see her finally.

She wasn't a woman—she was a teenager. Maybe seventeen, eighteen. Her clothing was ratty, filthy and torn. There was blood on the exposed skin of her legs and arms. But there was a frightening, peaceful look on her face as she stared at the Zanti. Then her eyes flickered and she saw Steve.

"Go away," she said gently. "This is one mistake I aim to pay for myself, with nobody's help."

Steve had no idea what she was talking about. He could only assume that she was delirious from fear. He moved forward, and she shook her head violently.

"No!" she cried, gesturing at the Zanti. "Look out!"

Glancing down, Steve saw that the Zanti had whirled around, and was now getting ready to attack him. It clearly considered him the more dangerous one. So much for détente! Steve dived past it as it sprang for him, twisting as it came toward him. Thanks to this, the Zanti's lunge missed, and it dropped lightly to the sand and dirt about ten feet away, its small thorax heaving as it struggled for breath.

That was an advantage, then. The Zanti, like Earth insects, could leap tremendous distances. But they had to rest a few seconds afterward. While it was recovering, Steve dashed to where the girl was still awaiting her fate and grabbed her arm. "Come on," he ordered. "We've got to get out of here."

"No," she cried, struggling to escape. "I have to stay and die, too. It's only right. It is."

"There have been enough deaths already," Steve told her, "and I don't plan on adding the two of us to the toll. Come on!" He jerked her to her feet.

She gasped again, and Steve spun around. The Zanti had skittered forward, and was preparing to attack again. Its mouth parts clicked together, and he could see drops of venom on them. That was how it had killed that man back at the car, Steve realized. A poisonous bite—and he would be next . . .

Without thinking, Steve scooped up a rock that was about a foot across. As the Zanti coiled to spring, Steve whirled the rock around and then slammed it down with all of his strength.

There was a sickening *crack!* as the Zanti's carapace shattered under the blow. The creature gave a shrill scream, and its long legs flailed momentarily before stopping forever.

Steve stared down at the crushed alien creature with dawning horror. He'd come out here specifically to try to talk to the Zanti. Instead of peace, he'd brought war on them all. He'd killed the monster without even consciously thinking about it. He'd had no option: it was either kill or be killed.

But what did this mean for the future of the human race now? Human had killed Zanti; what was going to happen when the rest of the Zanti found out?

Then he remembered that soon enough, there wouldn't be any *rest of the Zanti*. Grabbing the girl's hand again, he said, "We've got to get out of here now. The military's going to drop a missile on that ship. Come on!" He started to drag her back toward his Jeep.

"You've really blown it now, haven't you, Lisa?" the girl said, talking to herself. Her eyes were wide and frightened. The poor kid must be half-crazy with fear. "You tore it apart, looking for what held the seams together, and now you can't get it back together again." She gave him a terrifyingly sweet smile. "It's my doll," she murmured. "I've torn it apart, and it can't be fixed. Just like my life, all torn apart. Can't be fixed."

"We'll buy you a new one," he promised her, reaching the Jeep.

"A new doll?" Lisa asked brightly. "Or a new life? I'd only wreck it over again. That's all I know how to do."

"Well, I hope you know how to sit still and hold on," Steve replied. He pushed her into the passenger seat, then leaped into the driver's seat and started the jeep going. As fast as he could, he spun the vehicle around and started back toward the observation post in Morgue.

He could only pray that Hart had not launched that missile yet; otherwise this rescue would have been in vain. He heard a buzzing sound, and he looked back over his shoulder in alarm, expecting to see death heading toward him, in a plume of fire.

What he saw was even worse.

The Zanti ship had lifted off from where it had been perched in the rocks, and was moving slowly across the desert in his wake.

CHAPTER 12

ALL OF GENERAL Max Hart's dreams and hopes were collapsing about him. When he had first agreed to take the job as liaison with the Zanti, he'd been afraid that there would be a terrible price for humanity to pay for dealing with these creatures. He'd tried to still those fears by explaining Zanti behavior, excusing their rudeness, abruptness and unfriendliness. He'd tried to see their coercion as bargaining, and excused everything he could. He desperately wanted to believe that Earth's first contact with an alien species could go well.

And now, he was facing utter disaster. The Zanti had most likely killed at least one human being. Oh, they had been provoked, true enough, but their response was completely unreasonable. There had been no need for them to commit murder. And now it looked like Hill's worst fears were being realized—the inmates were escaping captivity, and he had no option but to risk a war of the worlds by shooting down the ship.

"General Hart?"

He looked down at the technician, who was holding out the headset. Hart slipped it on. "Steve? What is it?"

Grave's voice crackled back, and he could hear the fear in it. "The Zanti ship has taken off."

"We know," Hart answered. He glanced down at the low-level radar, which showed the blip appearing and disappearing. The Zanti had to know that the human tracking devices didn't work very well at low altitudes, and they were taking advantage of this.

"The Zanti are . . ." Steve's voice stopped, and then he sounded even more scared. "I had to kill one."

Hart's pulse almost stopped at that. "You what?" he asked weakly. *Dear God, it's worse than I thought . . .*

"It was about to attack me," Steve explained. "I saved the girl, though, and we're heading back. It was . . ." He broke off again. "Did they tell you where the ship is going?"

"No," Hart answered. He didn't want to think about the potential consequences of what Steve had done. It had to have been the missing regent that Steve had killed. Now there was no one to keep the prisoners in line, it seemed. "We've heard nothing official from anyone."

"We're almost clear of the target area," Steve reported.

"Drive as fast as you dare, Steve," the general told him. "War or no war, I may have to destroy that ship."

He handed back the headset, and turned to stare at the vague image on the radar screen. Major Hill moved to join him.

"Shall I get the president for you?" he asked. His eyes were shining, as if he were enjoying this. Given his feelings about the Zanti from the start, perhaps he was.

"No," Hart answered. There was no point, yet. "Do *you* know where that ship is going, Major?"

Hill pointed at the screen. "All I know," he said urgently, "is that they'll soon be out of missile range!"

Clutching at straws, Hart said, "Maybe they're going back to their own planet." It would be an ideal solution to the problem.

Hill snorted in derision. "Back to the planet that exiled them? Why would they want to do that? They can be free here!" He stared into Hart's face, and Hart could see the mounting fear in the major's eyes. "Destroy that ship, General! Advise the president to destroy the ship!"

Should he? Hart didn't know. It was all on his shoulders now, and suddenly he felt the weight of his age as if every year was a boulder on his back. He wanted to crumble under the pressure, but he knew that he couldn't. This was his task; it was why he'd been assigned to this mission. *The buck stops here*, he thought ironically. He *had* to decide.

The radar operator looked up, shocked. "General? The Zanti ship is coming straight toward us!"

Steve screeched the jeep to a halt outside the old saloon, and leaped from the vehicle. He glanced over his shoulder as he half helped, half dragged Lisa from the Jeep. The Zanti ship, only about fifty feet in the air, was moving toward the ghost town. It hummed and buzzed to itself, and appeared to be in little hurry. Pulling the girl along, Steve ran to the door, and slammed his hand on the entrance plate.

A moment later, the guard opened the door. He looked as if he were going to ask for identification, but Steve had no patience for the silly military game. He pushed past the man, hauling Lisa along, and then on into the main monitoring room.

Major Hill turned from the radar screen and glowered at the general. "It's too late now!" he yelled. "You waited too long! It's too close to fire a missile at it. We'd all get blown to eternity with it."

"Nice decor," Lisa murmured, still obviously not quite

with it. "Early computer age, with military trimmings."

Steve pushed her gently into a seat. "Stay there," he told her. "Keep out of the way." He'd filled her in on what was happening on the trip back, but he was unsure how much she'd understood. As he turned away from her, she suddenly grabbed his arm and held on to it.

"It's all our fault," she whispered. "Ben's and Jason's and mine. If we hadn't done what we did, gone into that area . . ." She shook her head. "I'm the one to blame for all this. I've started a war of the worlds!"

Steve looked at her with sympathy. He supposed that in one way, she might just be right about that. Maybe that was why she'd felt he should have left her to die. But he couldn't allow her to go on thinking like that. He was afraid she'd try to kill herself.

"It's not all your fault," he assured her. "I was the one who killed the Zanti. And they were the ones who demanded this crazy setup in the first place. They didn't have to kill Ben or Jason. They did it because they *wanted* to. You don't kill trespassers. You warn them off. At least, that's what anyone with a heart and real emotions does. The only ones to blame for all of this are the Zanti themselves." He gently pried her hands free. "Stay here and calm down," he told her. "I'm going to see what's going on. I'll see that you're taken care of. I promise. Trust me."

She was very pretty when she smiled, despite the dirt and the cuts and the hair that looked as if a family of rats had held a feud in it. "You know, I *do* trust you. I don't know why, because I've never really trusted anyone before."

Steve gave her what he hoped was a reassuring grin, and then went to join the general and Major Hill at the radar screen. What was happening now?

"We've lost it," the operator reported. "It's too low to track."

"Has it landed?" Steve asked, shaken.

Hart glanced at the door, and then jerked his head at the guard there. Understanding, the man ran out of the room. He was back a moment later.

"It's landed," the guard called. "It's on the roof above us."

Hart looked up. "On the roof?"

"It's a very small ship, Max," Steve explained. "The Zanti are only about a foot long. But they're lethal. They have some kind of poison sacs. According to Lisa, death is almost instantaneous if they bite you. They go for exposed skin."

"You think they aim to attack us?" Hart asked.

"Why else would they be here?" Steve replied. "They're desperate misfits who will only be free if they can get past us. I'm absolutely certain they're planning to attack us."

"Are we trapped?" asked Hill, staring up at the ceiling. "Do we sit here and wait for them? Or do we call down a missile that will kill all of them—and us with them?" He sounded on the verge of panic. Steve realized that Hill's worst nightmares were starting to come true. The man had never trusted the Zanti, and had been an outspoken opponent of this entire scheme all along. And now the Zanti were here, and ready to murder anyone who stood in their way.

"A missile won't be necessary," Steve said urgently. Though he certainly wanted to protect the human race, he'd prefer not to have to be a martyr to the cause. "They can be killed. They have hard shells, but they can be broken. I've done it."

"No!" Hill couldn't take any more. Steve turned, and saw Hill run toward the guard station. He snatched up an automatic rifle there and then ran past the guard and through the exit door. The bewildered guard turned to Hart for orders.

"Let him be," Hart commanded. "We've more important things to be concerned about now. Listen, everyone!" He raised his voice, and all eyes in the room turned to him. "Gentlemen and ladies, we are now in a war zone. All unnecessary tasks will cease. Prepare your weapons."

This was it, Steve realized. The war with the Zanti had begun.

Rushing outside, Hill was hardly conscious of what he was doing. All he could think was that his warnings had been ignored, his advice spurned, and now the thing he had feared all along had happened: the Zanti were attacking. He couldn't stand being cooped up inside of the saloon, just waiting for the inevitable; he had to *do* something, even if nobody else would.

He ran out into the street, hearing a loud buzzing sound from above. Looking back, he stood still, too shocked to even move.

The Zanti ship had crashed halfway through the roof of the old saloon. It was tilted at an angle, and part of the ship was within the broken shingles and rafters. Several small doors in the ship were open, and Zanti were pouring out. Some were dropping into the roof spaces created by the crash. Others were simply walking straight down the sides of the saloon. There weren't just dozens of the creatures—there had to be *hundreds* of them, swarming all over the building.

And they were incredibly repulsive, too. Just looking at them made Hill want to kill every last one of them. It was an instinctive disgust, a reaction formed from the pit of his being. Shocked, he raised the rifle, and moved forward.

But he caught his shin on the steps as he did so. The sharp pain in his leg made him cry out and fall forward. Holding the rifle didn't give him a hand to break his fall with, and his head slammed into the boards. His skull rang with the impact, and his vision blurred for a second. Putting out a hand, he tried to lever himself to his feet. As he did so, he felt something brush against his hand. He stared at it, willing his eyes to focus. Two large, evil eyes glared back at him. The antennae twitched, and then the Zanti leaped directly at his exposed face.

Hill barely had time for a scream.

Inside the control center, the military moved with determination. Hart was now on the radio to the outlying sentry posts. There was no call for them to be stopping people coming in, and they could be of more use here. "Flamethrowers should do it," he snapped. "Hand grenades. Rifles. Just *hurry*."

Steve nodded his approval, looking around for anything he might be able to use. He'd never even held a gun before in his life, and he'd probably be a terrible shot. But he wanted some kind of weapon for when the Zanti arrived.

"We have some of that stuff out in the stable," Hart informed him as he replaced the headset. "If we can get out the back way with a few men, maybe we can get ahold of it."

"Sounds good," Steve agreed. "Which way do we go?"

Hart gestured. The soldiers had now armed themselves with whatever was available, and were moving into position to cover all of the possible approaches to the building. Three men raced up the old stairs to the second floor. As Hart and Steve worked their way through the tangle of military, there was a howl from the stairs.

One of the men—he looked to be only a little older than Lisa—stumbled back, clawing at his neck. "Get it off me!" he screamed. "Kill it! Club it!" He spun around, and Steve saw that there was a Zanti on his back, grimly climbing toward the man's exposed neck.

The second man whipped up his rifle and then brought the butt down hard on the Zanti. It struggled for a moment, hissing, but its grip was broken, and it fell to the floor. The man then slammed the butt of his rifle down on the creature, shattering its body. With a high-pitched keening sound, the thing died.

And then another appeared on the floor, scurrying toward the men. One soldier fired at it, but missed, and it ducked behind an old case.

"It's begun," Steve whispered.

"We have to get out back," Hart said firmly. "They'll be hard to stop with just rifles and sidearms." He grabbed the arms of the nearest two soldiers, a man and a woman. "You two, with me. Come on, Steve." He headed toward the rear door, not looking back.

There was a scream from the stairs again, this time human. One of the guards fell backward, his body almost hidden under a mass of squirming, biting Zanti. The guard must have been dead before his body thumped onto the steps and rolled slightly. The Zanti leaped from the corpse, seeking further targets. Gunfire rang out as the humans tried to stop the avalanche of monstrosities.

Hart opened the rear door, and pointed. The stable was across the road, the door ajar. It would be a simple dash, and then they would have more weapons, ones that might be more effective.

Except there were Zanti everywhere. Several surged in the open door, dropping down from the wall above. The two soldiers opened fire, raking the doorway with sprays from their rifles. Broken Zanti bodies spun aside, but still more kept coming.

When the two soldiers paused to reload, Hart plunged past them. Steve followed. As he ran across the squelching remains of dead Zanti, several others threw themselves at him. Steve managed to bat aside the only ones to get close. One creature jumped onto the general's back, but the female soldier slammed the stock of her rifle into it, sending it spinning to the floor.

The man with her screamed as three Zanti landed on him and sank their poisoned fangs into his skin. Steve didn't stop—there was nothing that he could do for the man now.

And then they were in the stable. Racks of equipment sat there, and Hart grabbed a flamethrower. "Grenades," he yelled. The woman nodded, scooping several from an open case.

Then the Zanti came, and Steve couldn't keep his mind focused on any one thing. The female soldier threw her first grenade, and it exploded, taking out several invaders. But they kept coming. Steve snatched up a rifle, and somehow managed to get it working and firing in the right direction. Most of his shots missed, but now and then a Zanti body exploded.

And then Hart ignited the flamethrower. A huge, blazing gob of fire hurled out from it, and played across the closest of the Zanti. Their buzzing changed to screams as they fried.

And so it went on, and on, and on. . . .

Lisa stared all around her in shock. She'd been prepared to face her own death, but she was completely unprepared for any of this. Other people, innocent people, were screaming and dying as the alien monsters attacked them savagely. She saw the grotesque creatures climbing down the outside of windows, along the walls, down from the rafters, out from holes in the woodwork. They appeared to be everywhere.

Suddenly, she no longer wanted to die. Not like this, not by them. Snatching up a fallen rifle, she used it as a club, holding the barrel and slamming it down on Zanti after Zanti. She fought beside the few humans left alive in the room, her clothes splattered with Zanti fluids, her feet soaked in the offal from their corpses. She was hysterical, she knew, but she had no choice. She had to be with her fellow humans now, defending their right to live.

Hart's flamethrower cut a swath through the Zanti, and seemed to make them pause. But instead of giving up, they screamed out in their irritating buzzing voices, pressing forward again. The female soldier hurled out further grenades, which exploded. The street was pockmarked and burned, littered with the bodies of Zanti.

And still they came, streaming out of the main building. Did that mean that they'd killed everyone inside there? Steve felt a pang of guilt about Lisa. He'd promised to look after her, and he hadn't. His rifle was empty, and he tossed it aside, grabbing another from the rack and pouring shots into the wave of advancing invaders.

And suddenly there was another flamethrower in action, and more rifle fire. Steve was confused for a second, and then realized that it was the guards that Hart had called in from the perimeter. They were behind the Zanti, and the creatures were caught in a withering cross fire.

With the slaughter going so well, Steve made a break back toward the saloon, firing at anything that moved as he went. He ran inside, Zanti corpses squelching under his feet. He almost slipped several times, but he made it back into the control center.

There were only six people still alive there now. To his relief, Lisa was one of them. She was clubbing Zanti with a rifle, a terrible scowl on her face. Aiming carefully, Steve raked the attacking Zanti with bullets. He felt nothing but satisfaction as the aliens staggered, fell and died. Making his way across the room, he managed to reach Lisa's side.

"I told you I wouldn't abandon you," he said, over the roar of the gunshots.

"I guess you're one of the few people in this world who

really does keep his word,'' she managed to reply.

He grinned somewhat crazily as he continued to fight. Was it his imagination, or were there fewer of the Zanti attacking now?

A few minutes later, he realized that it hadn't been his imagination. There were just a dozen or so, still advancing on the humans. They were finally taking their toll. The rifle was hot in his hands, and then it stopped firing. Throwing it aside, he grabbed another from the body of a fallen soldier and kept firing.

Until, finally, exhaustingly, it was over. The only small black bodies around still moving were the wounded Zanti. Carefully, methodically, the soldiers went about the room, clubbing or shooting anything that still moved. But no more Zanti dropped from the ceiling, or crawled out of the woodwork. Panting, aching, Steve surveyed the room. There were corpses everywhere, many human, but mostly Zanti.

The battle was over, and the humans had won.

But the war was not yet done. . . .

CHAPTER 13

MORE SOLDIERS HAD arrived from an outlying base, and these had brought ambulances and trucks. Not that there were many soldiers for the ambulances to take. Anyone who'd been bitten by a Zanti was dead; it was as simple as that. But two men had been caught by friendly fire, and one man's arm had been torn by shrapnel from an exploding grenade, so they were seen to.

Using shovels, other soldiers started clearing the Zanti corpses from the control center.

"Burn them," Hart instructed. "There's plenty of wood in the old buildings. Make a pyre and burn every last damned one of those things." He looked older now, and more tired, but there was still steel in his spine and voice. To one of the lieutenants, he ordered, "Get a crew up to examine the ship on the roof. I want it taken down and removed for minute examination as soon as can be managed."

"Is there any hurry, General?" asked Steve.

"I don't know," Hart answered. "But if the Zanti don't know yet that we've killed all of their misfits, then they're bound to get suspicious soon enough. They're bound to try contacting their ship. And when they do, there will be no reply." He sighed. "Then they will have to retaliate. I'd rather the ship be elsewhere when they do. You, too, Steve. And the young woman."

"Do you think anywhere on Earth will be safe?" Steve asked, a hollow feeling in his stomach.

"Maybe not," Hart acknowledged. "But this is certain to be the least safe place of all. I want you out of here with the wounded. You both need hot showers, food and a rest."

"Oh, yes," agreed Lisa. Then she shook her head. "But I was one of the people who killed your sentry. Aren't you going to have me arrested?"

Hart grunted. "We'll worry about that later. Assuming that there will *be* a later."

Steve stared at her in surprise and apprehension. He'd forgotten all about the sentry that the car had hit. There had just been too many deaths since that had happened. He didn't know what her story was, but he somehow couldn't picture her as a killer. She was more of a victim. Well, she sounded like the thing she needed the most—aside from that shower— was a friend. And he'd promised he wouldn't abandon her. He'd see her through this somehow.

"Lisa, the general's right," he said gently. "It's time to leave here."

And then everything ceased. The speakers had suddenly come to life. Miraculously, the radio had not been harmed, despite all the violence. The radar, for example, was a smoking wreck, having been shattered by bullets. But the radio was still intact.

And the Zanti were speaking.

Everyone just looked at one another, numb with shock and

worry, as the metallic, irritating alien tones seeped from the speaker: "Lon faq i trin ob plam a klee o zona. Qui prel a bem klee o faq a venz ert yop a zan. Zan i vesti nom a quer a blan . . ." And so it went on.

Turning to the silent soldiers, Hart called, "Is there anyone here who can work the translator?"

One of the women nodded and moved to it. "It's still okay," she reported, tapping commands into the keyboard. She had to wipe Zanti blood from it first. As the message droned on, she managed to engage the translator.

This is it, Steve realized, his heart sinking. *The moment of truth. The Zanti must know by now we've killed their people.* Was this the final word, the death sentence on the human race? Rage, alien vengeance promised? Disgust? Despair? What? Steve discovered he was hugging Lisa tightly against his side, and she was clutching him ferociously for support. Hart had paled, and stood there helplessly, waiting to hear the word of doom.

"This is the commander of the government of the planet Zanti," the speakers said. "I speak to you from Zanti. You have destroyed our misfits. This we know." There was a short pause.

"We will not retaliate," the Zanti continued. "We never intended to. We knew that you could not live with such aliens in your midst. The Zanti long ago were killers. We still retain the poison sacs from those days. But a better philosophy prevailed, and we gave up the ways of violence. We are a peaceful people now. But the misfits were throwbacks who discovered that they could contemplate and perform acts of violence. We managed to capture them, but they were a plague to our race, a threat to the peace and stability that we formed. We were incapable of executing them, but they could not be allowed to live.

"It was always our intention that you destroy them, and

their guards, who were of the same, spoiled persuasion. We chose your planet specifically for that purpose. The arrangements made were deliberately provocative, to increase the certainty that you would not be able to get along with the misfits. The threats of our retaliation also were calculated to increase your paranoia. We are incapable of killing, but you are not. You are practiced executioners.'' There was another slight pause. ''We thank you for the service you have performed for our world.''

Lisa murmured, ''Practiced executioners!'' into Steve's ear. She seemed to understand perfectly the terrible compliment the Zanti had paid them.

Steve stared at the now-silent speakers in silence. So—it was over. There would be no war. The Zanti were incapable of such an act, in fact. They had simply used the human race to perform a necessary task that they were incapable of doing themselves. Steve knew he should be feeling elated, that in the end everything had worked out so well. The human race was safe, and they would not have to share any part of their world with the monstrosities from space. He should be feeling ecstatic.

But, as he led Lisa outside to a waiting transport, all he could feel was numbness. All around him, human corpses were being covered and taken away for burial. A few fires still flickered in the aftermath of the battle. And a great blaze had been started, the funeral pyre of the murdered—no, *executed!*—Zanti.

He should feel glad to be alive, and even more glad that the human race was not going to be annihilated. Maybe he would, later. But not now. Not after having paid such a terrible price.

It was a good thing that the Zanti were incapable of war— considering what they could do by being dedicated pacifists.

In the carnage and smoke, Steve helped Lisa into the truck, and then slid in beside her.

Right now, a shower was all he wanted out of life.

And, maybe, a promise that he wouldn't have nightmares about this day for the rest of his life. But nobody could promise him that. If they did, they'd be lying.

Throughout history, many societies have tried various forms of eradicating those members of their societies who have proven their inability or unwillingness to live sanely amongst their fellow men.

The Zanti have tried merely one more method. Neither better nor worse than all the others. Neither more human nor less human than some of the others. Merely . . . nonhuman . . .

TOR BOOKS

Check out these titles from Award-Winning Young Adult Author
NEAL SHUSTERMAN

TOR BOOKS

"A GREAT NEW TALENT. HE BLOWS MY MIND IN A FUN WAY."
—Christopher Pike

Welcome to the PsychoZone.

Where is it? Don't bother looking for it on a map. It's not a place, but a state of mind—a twisted corridor in the brain where reality and imagination collide.

But hold on tight. Once inside the PsychoZone there's no slowing down...and no turning back.

The PsychoZone series by David Lubar

❑ **Kidzilla & Other Tales**
  0-812-55880-4 $4.99/$6.50 CAN

❑ **The Witch's Monkey & Other Tales**
  0-812-55881-2 $3.99/$4.99 CAN